# Love and Belonging

## H J BURGESS

Published by H J BURGESS, 2023.

LOVE AND BELONGING

**First edition. May 27, 2023.**

Copyright © 2023 H J BURGESS.

ISBN: 979-8223457237

Written by H J BURGESS.

**Love and Belonging**
By Henry James Burgess

# Preface

Elizabeth watched in silence as her mother suffered a violent marriage and from an early age learned that looking after number one was the best way to deal with the hurt. Confusion about love, friendship and family would leave her damaged.

Her story begins in the East End of London; in the year 1953. It highlights attitudes, taboos, and expectations of that time. We follow her from childhood, through into a beautiful and independent woman. Experiencing personal loss and love in its raw, unyielding way. She makes one of the most damaging decisions of her turbulent life and protects herself with a web of lies and deceit. A shocking discovery creates a dilemma that threatens to destroy relationships and those closest to her to suffer the consequences.

# Chapter 1

A loud crack, a noise like a walnut being opened by nutcrackers at Christmas wrecked the silence. The China ashtray that had sat patiently waiting for a stubbed cigarette flew across the room and landed on the plain tiled floor. Father was in a rage again. Previously, he had kicked the small table by his chair; the ashtray had survived its flight but this time it was broken into several pieces. In a way it was fortunate that the table was there; his anger could have been towards my mother or me. She would no doubt offer another excuse for his frustration, defending his actions as normal and to be expected. Seemingly his life was not to his liking.

His job as a slaughterman working the permanent night shift at Smithfield Market was hard. It had its compensations though, as we always had a good cut of meat on the meal table, even the occasional chicken. Mother liked his shift work as she was able to see him off to work at 9 pm and then after I had gone to bed would read her favourite books. Love triangles and the like. Refined people dressed in exquisite clothes, living in large stately houses with extravagant lifestyles. These fantasies took her mind away from the reality of my father's homecoming.

He finished work at 4 am but spent the next two hours supping ale in 'The Black Swan' the public house next to the market which was kept open just for the meat men. The locals called it the 'The Mucky Duck'. Occasionally, a London taxi driver, theatre usher or off-duty policeman could be found here. Everyone who wanted cheap meat went there as most of the men traded a joint or two of meat for cigarettes or another glass of ale. It was a perk of the job to take home something each night. The chickens were still in feathers and their eyes popped out at you. The cigarettes were foreign; Mother disliked them and often said she would never go to France if they all smelt like that.

Mum was a simple woman with simpler ways. Her ambition had been quashed by my father many years ago. I remember as a small child her singing as she rocked me gently to sleep. Her excitement when I completed my first day at school. We had strawberry jam on chunky doorstep slices of fresh bread. She would hold the loaf to her breast and cut the slices off the top. A dangerous thing to do but made it easier as the bread was so fresh it fell apart if cut on the breadboard.

Happier times when we all went to the cockle sheds, on the edge of Margate beach for our afternoon tea. Nothing compares to a plate of cockles with lots of white pepper and malt vinegar splashed over. I did not like the whelks though; it was like eating rubber with little taste. Dad would disappear for an hour while Mum and I would collect whole shells off the beach. Staying in a caravan for our holidays was great fun then, but now things had changed. Somewhere along the way Dad had become a bully and Mum had lost the will to live.

Mum rose from her crouched position, crossed the room, and picked up the broken ashtray. Looking at the table it was obvious it had not survived either and its remnants were lifted out into the garden.

'I want some breakfast' he roared, then slumped into the armchair and went to sleep.

Mum started cooking his bacon and eggs along with fried bread. Very soon it was ready, and she called to him. He did not move, so was prodded to wake him. Nervously she stood back while he opened his eyes.

'Where is it?'

'It's on the kitchen table with your cup of tea' she replied nervously.

He staggered across the room and supported by the door handle passed through into the kitchen.

'It's bloody cold and look at all this fat; it's been set for ages'

'It's only been a minute or two' she tried to explain.

Placing the kettle back on the cooker, she lit the gas and turned around. His clenched fist buried itself between her breasts with such force as to knock her across the room and she hit the wall with a resounding thud and fell to the floor.

'I'm going to bed, wake me at 12 o'clock, I'll have lunch at the pub'

With no marks to show for her ordeal Mum could never get anyone to believe what happens in our house. He knew this and always hit her where it would not show.

After tidying the house, she sat in the garden saying nothing to me; book in hand she quietly read for about an hour. I was unable to wait any longer. Slowly approaching I cast a shadow over her. She looked up at me and smiled.

'Are you all right mum?' I quizzed.

'Yes dear' she replied, as she stretched out her arms and I sank into them.

'What are we going to do my darling Beth?' she whispered.

I had no answer, so just held her tightly.

'Go and play with your friends now, as I've got to wake up your father' she urged, patting me on the head as I stood up.

'I do love you Mum' and I kissed her on the forehead.

Within seconds I was outside in the street. It was 1953 and a new Queen was in the making. Our street was decked out with tables borrowed from St. Stephen's Church Hall and some chairs from Robert Petersons, my old junior school. There was to be a street party and most of my friends had already been busy blowing up balloons and making streamers from rolls of crepe paper since incredibly early.

Mrs Andrews from number 47 came over to me.

'What do you think?' she said excitedly and continued

'I've tried my best to make it look like a million dollars

I didn't know what that meant, so just agreed with her, then made my way to the far side of the street to find good old Mr. Peacocks' wooden fence being pulled down and put across the end of the street. A big sign had been placed on a pole telling people not to take their cars through.

'Do you want to help?' called a voice.

I looked around.

'You can help me lay out the plates if you want'

'Can I?' was my eager reply.

The man was not known to me but seemed nice.

The party was due to start at 4 pm and I figured out that I should sit opposite the red brick house. It did not have a number just a name, but I could not read it. Someone told me it was in Spanish. The house had new shiny black gates. My father did not like them or the man who lived there, Mr. Jamieson.

'He's got a bloody cheek' he had once said.

'We all had to give up our railings and gates during the war effort to make armaments and here he was wasting good metal on such an extravagance'

I did like his son David though. He was a little older than me and I thought he was lovely. He had dark features and dark eyes; his mum looked foreign. I secretly hoped he would be outside his house, and I made two reservation cards and placed them next to each other on the table.

I finished my work and with a great bounce in my step went home to change. I wanted to wear my new pink dress with sparkles sewn into the neckline, so hurried along the road. It was about 2 pm and Father would still be at the pub.

I expected to find Mum busy in the kitchen but as I opened the back door she called out from upstairs. Quickly, I rushed to her, only to find their bedroom scattered with clothes. His were still hanging in the wardrobe but mums were hastily being thrown into a suitcase that lay open on the bed. We only used the cases when we were going on holiday to the caravan, so I was confused as nothing had been mentioned.

'What's going on?' I asked

'No time now to explain, your stuff is in those bags on the landing, grab them and put them by the front door'

'But'

'Don't argue, just do it'

The urgency of her voice said a lot and I dutifully carried them down. Mum followed and within a blink of an eye, we were soon making our way along the front path.

'Oh my God, where's the taxi?' her face full of torment as she looked in both directions.

'The street is closed for the party' I called out.

Mum was already moving towards the corner, almost running but for the weight of the case and bag, she was holding as I followed at a distance. My thoughts were torn between the party and my seat next to David and my mother's erratic behaviour. I started counting the seats from his place, four, five, six and so it was, I was leaving him. I thought of Father coming home and us not being there. What would he think, the mess in the house and no clean overalls for his night shift? Mum would be in trouble, that is for sure.

A group of mothers watched as we passed by them. I heard one of them say

'It's about time'

Another agreed and added

'Well, I would have gone years ago'

One of my bags was heavy and I changed hands to try and balance the weight. My arms felt painful, and I was starting to wheeze as my asthma took over. The taxi driver called me to hurry as the meter was running.

A friend of mine, Janine ran over as I struggled the last few yards and helped with the bags.

'Where are you off to then?' her innocence clear in her voice.

'Don't know yet'

'I do love surprises, don't you?' she quipped.

5

I did not have time to answer her and was frogmarched into the taxi by Mum. The look on Janine's face changed, her smile had gone and replaced with alarm. I looked back through the window and could make out several of my other friends who had come to Janine's call. Their gestures bade me stay. I did not want to leave them, but Mum was on a mission.

Once we were underway, she turned to me.

'I owe you an explanation' she said calmly.

Her hands gripping mine and looked directly at me with her wretched face.

'You know how things are with your father; well, I think its best if we have a little break at my sisters by the sea'

I did not know what to say and just smiled. Yes, I knew exactly why we were leaving but could barely bring myself to speak, although I did say

'He could decorate the front room while we're away'

Mum did not reply, just continued to stare out of the taxi. I suppose the thought of him decorating was a bit ridiculous as Father hated the house and hated decorating even more.

The journey seemed endless, and I had time to reflect on what was happening. We were alone now, and I was not sure whether Mum would cope, or that I could support her. It was a very brave thing she had done but I felt she had not worked out the future at all. Would he come after us or maybe he would be glad of the peace and quiet? I was not a quiet child and now as a teenager was probably more trouble than I was worth. Maybe it was my fault. My head was full, and I started to cry. Mother cradled me and her soft hand stroked my hair.

We soon pulled up outside Plaistow train station. The driver's husky voice echoed into the booking hall

'Good luck missy' he said placing our bags on a trolley.

We scurried along as steam shot out from the side of the engine backing onto the carriages already waiting on platform 4 southbound. A man noticed us struggling and offered to help.

'No' she shrieked sternly.

The man stood back in some amazement. Hesitating a little, Mum continued

'I'm sorry, but no thank you'

It seemed to offer the man some release from his shock.

We boarded and I found a window seat. With our bags stowed in the racks above our heads, Mum sat opposite.

'Why wouldn't you let that man help us?'

'Well, I should think not, what would your father think, me talking to strange men on a train station, whatever next'

I looked at her with a straight face; she looked at me. Then, as the train edged forward with a jolt, we both burst out laughing. It was the first time I had seen her laugh for many years. If leaving home was this much fun, we were sure to be all right.

# Chapter 2

The next 2 years passed very quickly, and our fortunes were still not made. My schoolwork improved steadily, and I felt quite secure. Father was a distant memory; he had never found us, and I am not sure he even looked. Mum was looking older and spent a lot of time every morning in front of the mirror.

'Never tells the truth' She mumbled to herself

I think maybe the mirror was right though, her face was drawn, and she had been losing weight for some time. I would guess Mum was about 12 stone for most of her life. Now I suspect she only weighed a mere 7 or more. A remark from a newfound friend prompted Mum to visit the doctor; something she rarely needed to do. After a referral to a hospital specialist, we waited for about 2 weeks for the results.

The postman was not a frequent visitor to our house, so made a big thing about the large brown envelope.

'Could be a cheque from Vernon's pools' he said cheerfully.

Laughing in response Mum waved to him and closed the door, placed the letter on the table and slid into her bedroom. It seemed like an eternity before she came out but was probably only a few minutes.

'Well,' I urged

'Well open it then'

'All in good time my child'

She paused for a moment

'Why don't we put the kettle on?'

I could not understand why the envelope remained tightly sealed. If it was my letter, then it would have been torn open before the postman had turned his back. The kettle boiled and the tea was brewed. Out came the best cups, our only cups should I say. We had not spent much on things for the house since we arrived, money being tight. After the first sip of the tea Mum opened the letter. Mum never looked as old as she did now and gracefully took both my hands into hers. An empty feeling came over me, my stomach pulled in as I drew breath. What could it be?

'It's what I had feared my darling child'

'What?'

I could see it was difficult for her to speak.

'The results show I have a problem'

'What problem?

I paused a while, then in a raised voice

'I am old enough to know the truth, please tell me'

'Yes, you're quite right; you are almost a woman now'

'Come to the point mum'

'Well, I had a small lump in my breast and according to the doctor the problem has spread to other parts of me'

I was horrified at this news. Mum stood up and pulled a sheet of paper from her bag and passed it to me.

'I've made a list of things you must do when I'm not here'

I looked at her in total amazement.

'What do you mean when you're not here?'

'Well, I think its best if we are prepared for the worst'

'You think you are going to die, don't you?'

'The doctor told me what to expect so I've made this list'

'So, you knew all this time'

I began shouting as my anger spilt out at her. Why didn't I get told before? Why now?

'Let me see the letter'

I snatched it from her. Maybe there had been a mistake. Maybe there were two people with the same name. I searched for answers, but none came. Moments later, I stood up and ran to the window. Looking across from here I could see people going into the Church of All Saints; somewhere we have not been lately.

'Quickly, let us go to the service, God will have something to say' I ranted.

'No, it's not that easy' she said in a low voice, a tone of acceptance.

I was not comforted and still needed to know more.

'I've spoken to the doctors, and I left it too late'

'Too late; too late for what?'

'I found the lump last year, but I hoped it would go away on its own'

'Your stupid bitch' I screamed.

'They don't just go away'

I fell and laid my head on her lap.

'Didn't mean to swear mum, I'm so sorry'

'You're upset angel'

Mum thought it had been for the best, but she did not know me well enough. Considering the life, we had before and my feelings of loss at not seeing my father, even if he was a bully was overwhelming. Then there was David, a fantasy I know but it did not stop me crying every night for months. She had not noticed any of this. Maybe I covered my feelings well.

I had grown up under her nose and neither of us realised it. My mind swirling, I thought of myself. I had lost one parent and now she was going to go: leaving me alone. How would I cope? A girl needs her mum especially now at age 15. I was being selfish, just like my father. Was this the price she paid for leaving him? Was it my fault for not asking how she was more often? Why couldn't we go to the service and ask God to help, that is what he is there for, isn't it?

'Let me put the kettle on and freshen up the pot' she calmly said as she went into the kitchen.

I called out to her.

'Is that all you can think of at a time like this? You're so British, I could kick you'

'It never got your father anywhere' she wryly replied.

As she returned said

'There should just be enough milk left in the jug'

Placed the teapot on the tray and sat down in the chair.

The room was becalmed, and she had lost that aged appearance. The majestic movements of picking up the sugar bowl and topping the cups left me in no doubt, God had not forgotten her. I felt him calming everything, it was so reassuring. Even with this tranquillity, I needed to ask.

'How long?'

'I don't know yet, maybe three years, three months, or three weeks'

I realised now I should not have asked but since I had, it seemed only right that we continue to talk about it. Leaning alongside the chair I picked up the piece of paper from the floor where I had thrown it.

'This list, what shall I do with it?'

'Well, nothing just now, let us drink our tea and then go for a walk'

Outside our rented house the seasons came and went but now everything seemed to be in full bloom. It was usual for me to hold her arm for much of the time when we went out, but today I gripped it harder than ever. The great thing about our relationship was sharing almost every moment of our time together, but what of the future? I was so frightened.

Mum helped me carry out most of the tasks on the list over the next few weeks and with her dividend at the Co-op along with the insurance, the funeral costs would be covered. She did not want anything fancy; it was not her way. It was whilst we were at the funeral directors that I breached the subject.

'What shall we do about Father?'

'Best we say nothing to him' she said in a soft voice.

I knew it was unlikely that he would come to the funeral, but I felt he should know. Maybe pay his respects and all that.

'All right then, but do you think he should be told?'

'No, definitely not and let that be the end of it'

The next day we made our way to Aunt Mabel's house, another relative of Mum living in a small village near Faversham in Kent and found ourselves sitting in her front parlour; a room kept for visitors. A small room made even smaller by the sheer volume of ornaments and collectables that adorned every nook and cranny.

'That one is from India, Bombay I think' Aunt Mabel pointing to the ornate figurine of a bird perched on the shelf above the empty canary cage.

'My dear departed brought that home after one of his exploits. He told me he won it in a game of cards with the captain of a ferry. Heaven knows what he must have been doing'

As she continued to be amusing, I thought of my father and his dead chickens.

'So, you think you will settle here with me then?' she said

'No, I ......'

'You will have to help around the house, you know, make yourself useful'

Mum placed her arm around my shoulder and reassured me

'I just need to go home and settle a few things, but I will join you soon. You will be all right here with your aunt'

The decision had obviously been made. I felt rather annoyed by this lack of involvement, but I could see in Mum's face this was what was for the best. I would have to get used to it. Before much else was mentioned a girl entered the room.

'This is Maureen, my daughter'

Aunt Mabel ushered her into the middle of the room and urged her to shake hands. She appeared to be very embarrassed by this. She wore a very pretty dress almost the same as my party dress. Her hair was pushed up and held in place by a comb with a small butterfly.

'I don't think we have met before, have we?'

I was relieved that she spoke first and replied that we had not unless it was when we were young. Moving forward my mum kissed me and gave half a hug.

'You're both the same age, so you should get on well together' were her parting words as she prepared to go home.

Taking my hand, Maureen stroked it reassuringly and in a soft voice suggested that we look at my room upstairs. I was still a little upset by all this happening so quickly. So, hesitantly I followed her out of the room. Although the parlour was small the rest of the house was enormous, and it was quite a trek to the upper floors and the bedrooms. As I entered the room a warm feeling came over me.

'I like this, I like this lot'

Maureen smiled.

It was cosy and as I am not a tall person the low ceilings did not bother me. There were two windows, one facing the courtyard where a grassed area fringed the concrete paving. The other view was spectacular. The manicured gardens fell away down a long slope and dissolved into a natural area which was overgrown with flowers mingling in the tall grasses. Beyond this, I could just make out something glistening.

'What's that down there?' I queried

'My rooms above yours on the next floor, you can get a better view from there'

So up we went to her room, the stairs were much narrower and the walls less distinctive like the lower floors that had fancy door frames and plasterwork around the ceilings.

'See, I told you so'

'It's a river'

'Well, I would call it a stream; it often dries up'

The water ripples danced over the stones just beneath the surface. A new picture emerged every second, a new delight for the onlooker. I could see a building beyond the stream and a group of trees.

'What's that over there?'

'A boy's school' she giggled

'Have you got a boyfriend there?' I asked.

14

She continued to giggle and passed me a scrapbook.

There on the first page was a picture of a boy with his trousers down, his bottom on display.

'Goodness, is he your boyfriend?'

'Not saying'

My embarrassment obviously showing, she turned the pages for me. There were several pictures, but none were so explicit. There was also a girl, but Maureen closed the book and replaced it beneath her bed.

'Tomorrow is their sports day; do you want to go and check them out?'

'Well, yes I think so'

David had been the only boy I had any thoughts for but here I was contemplating meeting so many, all in one go. I looked forward to tomorrow and giggled a little. The initial shock of arriving here and being told it was to be a permanent thing still rang in my head, but the prospects looked better all the time.

'I'm back at my school next week. I suppose you will be going there too'

I had not thought of school, and it would be yet another bridge to cross.

The next day Maureen insisted she helps me get dressed and gave me one of her outfits to wear.

'Make-up is a must' she suggested as she applied far too much.

I only had a little lippy and some eye shadow. Dressed to kill we set off to the school boundary.

'I know just the place from where to watch them; a tree right by the playing field fence, just out of sight of the pavilion' she suggested and continued

'Teachers could be there, so we don't want to be seen'

Except for the boys, I thought.

The wait was worth it. A couple of lads came up to the fence and started showing off. Wrestling and pushing each other to the ground for our amusement. I took a fancy to the tall boy; I think Maureen did as well. In time, the playful display ended, and they leaned on the fence to talk. Our interests were with Jonathon, his mate Malcolm was all right but did not have the looks. It did not take long for me to be offered a date and I agreed to meet Jonathon on Saturday. I think Maureen was a little disappointed and reluctantly said

'Let us make a foursome'

I thought this was a great idea, as the prospect of meeting this lad on my own terrified me.

On the way home Maureen spoke a lot about the boys from the school.

'I've been with quite a few'

She seemed pleased with herself. I was not sure what she meant, maybe a kiss, maybe more. I just nodded in agreement.

'My first time made me sick, and I cried all night' she continued to expand on her claims.

I could not ask her to explain in detail, things like that were never mentioned at my old school. In fact, it all seemed rather personal to talk about, but it did excite me a little to hear Maureen.

Later we went upstairs. It had been an unusual day; one I would not forget in a hurry. I was ready for sleep and when alone I lay on the bed and went out like a light.

# Chapter 3

Saturday arrived and we prepared ourselves as before. There was no sign of them at the agreed time of 10 o'clock so we just hung around the marketplace in the town, keeping an eye out for them. It was almost 11 o'clock when they appeared so we were none too pleased. No excuses were offered, and they acted as though nothing was wrong. Maureen was upset and refused to talk to her boy. Mine put his arm around me and kept nibbling my ear. I did not like it at first, but it made me feel less annoyed.

After about half an hour we all went to the park nearby, armed with several bottles of cider. Jonathon had passed for 18 when he went into the off-licence and had spent all his money for the week, or so he says. After much larking about and drinking the cider, we sat down in a bit of a dip in the ground and started talking.

'What do you think of us then?' Maureen asked

The boys both looked at her and then at me. I could not believe her asking such a forward thing. We have only just met them, and she asked that. Much to my surprise, they both replied at the same time.

'You're great'

It appears they were on the same wavelength.

'Do you say everything together?' I asked tentatively.

'Most things' answered Malcolm

'We do everything else together as well' chipped in Jonathon.

'Do you?' Maureen looked intrigued

From where we sat no one could see us. Maureen seemed to realise this and began kissing Malcolm quite hard on the lips. I imagined she had been here before. Their petting was getting carried away and he had his hand on her breast. I stood up and was ready to go but was asked to sit down by Jonathon. He seemed so nice about it that I did not refuse. I looked at Maureen as she came up for air.

'You will like it, go on kiss him' She barely had time to say it before she was back with Malcolm.

'Can I kiss you then?' asked Jonathon as he pulled me to him. We kissed and I let him put his arms around me. I must confess it was nice and this carried on for some time.

The cider had all been drunk by now and I think I had too much. My head was swimming a little and I let Jonathon touch my breasts outside of my dress. He whispered that I should look at the other two who were now partly undressed. Maureen was sitting on Malcolm and rocking forwards and backwards. She looked towards us.

'Go on, you have a go, it's really good'

This was unbelievable and I did not know what to do or say.

Jonathon's hand moved up inside my dress and found my bare breasts. They were small and he rolled a nipple between his finger and thumb. I do not know whether it was the drink or my inquiring mind that let me allow him to do this. I felt quite at ease with things, and we lay there for some time.

Maureen had been very vocal in the last few moments, making all sorts of funny noises. She stood up and came over, sitting down next to me. Jonathon and I were excited, and Maureen could see this.

'Would you like a condom?'

'Yes please'

Jonathon held out his hand after releasing his command of my nipples. Maureen kept hold of it. I was not sure what would happen next but something inside my head said go with the flow. Jonathon brought his hand back but instead of resuming as before, he slid it between my legs and touched me. I offered no resistance and Maureen opened the little packet.

'Are you ready then, it's now or never?'

I looked at her and then at him. It seemed so right. He moved away from me a little and pulled off his trousers and pants. It was the first time I had been so close to such a thing. I had seen one of the boys at our school doing a wee in the girl's toilet when theirs was broken but this was different.

It was soon over, and Maureen leaned across and kissed me on the forehead. We all stood up and Jonathon put his trousers back on. I was amazed that no one saw us but if I could not see them, it was obvious, they could not see us.

Malcolm checked the bottles to see if any drink had been left and threw them into the bushes. I could not think straight, and Maureen suggested we go home. The lads were quick to disappear after asking us to meet again next Saturday, at the same time. Maureen did mention the confusion earlier and they admitted they did it to see how keen we were. Bloody cheek I thought, but after what had just happened, I could not say much. Walking home we chatted about the boys, and I had to admit it was rather good. It did hurt a little but with an audience, I was not going to say anything, I was already embarrassed enough. By the time we reached the market, another boy started to talk to us.

'Saw you down at the park' he declared

'Did you now?'

Maureen smiled at me

'What do you think you saw then?' I asked, my heart racing

'Everything' he said in a very cocky voice

She matched his confident manner with her own style, almost like a schoolteacher.

'Would you like some of the same then?' she was taunting him now.

'Bet you've never actually done it' she mocked him terribly

'Of course, I have, loads of times'

'Well, prove it then'

I stood back; their tone was getting rather heated.

'Follow me'

Maureen pulled at his jacket, and he strode after her into the lady's toilet. I kept close as I followed them. We all piled into a cubicle, and he sat on the toilet with the lid down. Maureen stood directly in front of him, and I pressed myself into the corner by the door.

'Go on then, she challenged him.

Lifting her skirt to expose herself; she had discarded her knickers earlier. He leant forward, fumbling aimlessly at her crease. He momentarily looked at me and then at her. The cubicle was hot, and I fought for air. I was so excited my pulse was electric. He kept this position for several moments. Suddenly, she pushed him away.

'You need more practice boy'

'Come on Beth, we've got to go'

With that, the door was opened, and we were gone.

I looked back as we reached the corner, and I could see him running like the wind in the other direction.

'Shall I tell his mates he was rubbish?' said Maureen

I did not answer her and kept walking. Our arms linked together just like I did with Mum. Aunt Mabel greeted us as we entered the house.

'Had a good day, you two?

'Yes, thank you' I murmured

'I'm going for a bath, are you coming?

Maureen beckoned me and we left the room.

Later, as I was drying my hair she came into my room. Closing the door behind her she bounced onto my bed.

'I didn't realise you were a real virgin'

I looked at her and nodded in agreement.

'What do you think of it then?'

There was urgency in her voice. I did not want to talk about it, but it was obvious she was not going to leave without dissecting everything.

'It hurt me at first'

'That's normal but how do you feel now you've lost it?'

'Fine' I replied but it was not quite true.

'You have to practice getting it right, you know'

I hope she did not mean I should give in to every boy I met. I still could not answer my own questions. Why Jonathon and why only just after meeting him? Was it the cider? I could have blamed the drink very easily, but I was not fooling anyone really, least of all myself. She was so grown up and I listened intently to her as she relayed some of her conquests to me. It was obvious now that something should have happened when I had sex with Jonathon. It had felt nice but the way she went on meant I had missed something significant. The way she talked was alien to me.

'You speak a foreign language I'm sure' I said

'You do need help' she said scornfully

'I will teach you if you like'

'You, but how?'

'Not now' we'll start tomorrow'

She stood up and kissed me directly on my lips, and 'By the way you can call me Mo' then left the room. I soon slipped into an uneasy sleep and never went down for supper.

I woke early about 5 am; the birds were still congregating for their mass departure from the telegraph wires that crossed the rear courtyard. I felt uncertain about myself and lay wondering what was missing yesterday. Mo had been quite amazing and had opened so many questions. Then, without knocking Mo entered the room and caught me spread-legged.

'I won't have to teach you that lesson then, but do be careful; you don't want the rest of the house to know what you're doing'

With that, she went out of the room.

During the following week, we spent a lot of time together in her room playing with her new tape recorder. Most of her recordings were quite poor quality as they were copied off the radio. The music was immensely popular with us kids, much to the annoyance of most adults. The time soon passed, and Saturday arrived. The weather was especially hot even early in the morning. After a light breakfast, Mo urged me to get ready. I picked out a cream dress with flowers on the short sleeves and a pair of brown shoes. Mo took one look and told me to get them off.

'I'm not going out with you looking like that'

I did not have many clothes and Mo offered to let me wear something from her wardrobe.

'Try this'

She handed me a skirt and I held it up against myself.

'Goodness, I can't wear this, it's far too short'

'Don't be silly'

I reluctantly tried it on, and Mo passed me a top that resembled a waistcoat. No sleeves and just two buttons at the front. I was surprised to find that I looked good and agreed to wear them.

'Something is not quite right' Mo looked puzzled

'Here try this'

She handed me a wide black shiny belt with a large silver buckle.

'That's better'

I loved the outfit and could not wait to go to town to see the boys again. Mo still was not happy though and suggested I remove my bra as you could see most of it and it did not do justice to the top. I did not mind leaving it off, but as I am only small, I felt a little less than perfect without my padding though. We arrived in the marketplace early and knew the boys would be some time yet, even if they were on time.

'Let us have tea in the cafe' Mo suggested

We ordered the drinks, and both had a cake. Mo asked for the creamiest in the place and we duly sat in the window to watch the people go past. The boys arrived early, and we could see them clearly, but the windows of the cafe reflected the morning sunlight, so they were unaware of us watching them. Malcolm seemed very agitated and kept kicking the ground. I have noticed boys do that. Jonathon seated on a bench lit a cigarette. I did not know he smoked. Mo finished her cake and wanted to meet up, but I always eat slowly and continued to nibble the edges of mine. Wiping the crumbs from her mouth we left the cafe and walked slowly towards them. I still had half my cake, now in a bag taken from the counter.

As the boys caught sight of us, Jonathon quickly threw the cigarette to the floor and twisted his foot on it.

'On time today then' Mo said sarcastically and prodded Jonathon in his ribs.

I still think she fancied him and did not seem to acknowledge Malcolm standing close by.

'What are we doing today?' Malcolm asked defensively

'Don't know' Mo said as she kicked the floor.

I was amused by this and giggled. The boys looked at me wondering what the hell I thought was funny. Jonathon suggested going to the park, so Mo grabbed his arm and started to walk on. I was quite annoyed at this. He was my boyfriend, and she had no right. Malcolm walked after them, leaving me to catch them up. Before I reached them, I heard Aunt Mabel calling me from the other side of the square. I stopped and she rushed over to me.

'I'm so glad I found you' she wheezed and tried to catch her breath.

'Auntie, what's the matter?'

Taking my arm, she led me back to the wooden bench and we sat down.

'Come on' cried Mo and waved to me.

'Never mind them; I've got something important to tell you'

Auntie looked serious and she explained that my mum had taken ill, and I was to travel back home straight away. We were soon at my auntie's house and started to pack a travel bag. I was very worried for my mum and did not waste time changing clothes. I hoped Mum does not mind, she has strong views on how people dressed, and this outfit did not cover much.

23

A taxi had been called and as I waited patiently the telephone rang in the hallway. It made me jump as not many people had a telephone, so I was not used to the sound. Auntie answered it.

An old London black cab pulled up outside and replaced the handset on the phone, auntie went out and started to speak to the driver. I followed her and put my bag on the open luggage rack next to the driver's cab. The driver came around and took it off, placing it on the ground.

'You're not going now my dear' Auntie said sheepishly.

'Why?'

'Let us go inside'

I made my way into the house. Auntie came in and put the kettle on. I knew something was wrong, but what? The making of tea seemed to precede bad news. Before it had boiled Auntie explained that Mum had not survived the night and I no longer needed to go. I wanted to but everything had been sorted out for me. I desperately wanted to say goodbye to her, but so much remained unsaid. I could not wait for the tea and went to my room. I must have cried myself to sleep as the next thing was Mo crashing into the room.

'I'm so sorry'

Being aware of my plight, she held me in her arms for ages. She stayed with me for most of the evening and fetched my supper on a tray. I did not eat much and a little later, Mo stood up

'Bless you my darling' and went to her room.

It must have been about 2 am when Mo entered my room again. I had been crying and hearing this had come down to comfort me. She asked if she could get into my bed. I needed someone and welcomed her warm body close to mine. She never spoke, just cuddled up to me. My mum had often allowed me into her bed when I was younger, and this reminded me of those happier times. I began to think of all the things I could no longer do with her and started to cry again. Mo held me tightly and kissed me on the cheek. I do not know why but I kissed her full on the lips. She responded and kissed me again. This time gently and I was aroused. Maybe it was my grief or maybe something else that took over my emotions, but I could not stop myself from fondling her soft body, my hands caressing her all over. She placed her hand on my bare breasts and fondled them to awaken something inside me. Urgently, I took her hand and pushed it downwards into my threads of golden hair. She held back momentarily and then touched me. Her fingers soothed my ache. I turned to her, and we kissed like lovers do. For hours we shared each other until daylight crept across the bedroom.

# Chapter 4

A week passed quickly, and I found myself at the graveside. Freshly mown grass scented the air and made my nose start to itch. I sneezed loudly and everyone looked at me. They did not frown but smiled sympathetically. The sermon was long, and I became quite ill, almost falling into the open ground. Mo gripped my arm firmly and I was glad she had travelled down with me. Auntie had not been able, as her arthritic knee had flared up some days earlier. I carried a message from her though.

'Tell your mum that I will look out for you, and she need not worry herself'

I was not sure when I was supposed to deliver it, so at the end of the service I remained at the graveside. I asked Mo to wait by the iron gates and gave Mum my last farewell, promising to be a good daughter. A little robin flew down, settling on the mound of earth alongside me. A thought crossed my mind; maybe Mum has come back as a bird. I shuddered and ran to the car waiting to take us back to another relative's house. Mo and I squeezed into the back seat along with someone I did not know. He had some awful aftershave on, and I rolled down the window to get some air. Mo smiled at him, but I just breathed loudly.

At the house, I was introduced to a lot of people claiming to be related to me. Uncle this, and Auntie that, it was so confusing. Where had all these people been previously? Why had I never seen them before? I did not have a clue. The cake was fresh, and I had several slices. Mo remarked that I was eating for two; we did laugh. Later, I got talking to one of these newly found relatives and it became clearer why we had never met before. My father had created so much bad feelings within the family when he married Mum that everyone stopped coming to the house. I did not ask what it was about but made a promise that I would try and keep in touch with them. Mo and I were given separate rooms at the far end of this rambling old house. It was quite spooky, and I think Mo would have preferred to sleep in my room. She did not though, and I was soon asleep covered with a thick woollen blanket.

The next day we had a good breakfast of porridge and poached eggs on thickly buttered toast. I loved the eggs, but the porridge was too salty. Mo did not say anything, but her face told a story or two. I tapped her leg under the table and we both giggled.

'You're both in high spirits today, that's good to see' remarked my newly found Auntie Edna.

Mo dropped her head apologetically; she obviously thought it was not right to be jolly at a time like this.

'Life goes on' I quipped, and they both agreed.

We packed up our few bits and were soon making for the car parked outside; another relative had offered to run us to the station. We said our goodbyes, hugging everyone that came to see us off.

At the train station, we sat on a long seat. It was Saturday morning, and the platform was deserted except for a little robin hopping in and out of the flower bed. I pointed to the bird and told Mo what I had thought yesterday. She looked serious and explained her grandmother was a fortune teller in a travelling show many years ago. She was long since dead, but Mo remembered something she had said before she died.

'We all come back as something else and occasionally as a guardian angel'

'No, I don't believe you'

'It's true, my granny was no faker'

'Well, if that is the case then that little bird is my mum'

'Don't mock things you don't understand'

Mo was still serious, and I did think for a moment that there could be some truth in it.

'Okay, just for you I will not joke anymore but I'm still not convinced'

Standing up, Mo kissed me on the forehead as the train juddered to a halt. The seats on the train were filthy, so we placed a newspaper down to save our clothes. Unfortunately, the print from the paper came off and made a mark on both our outfits; so much for being careful. The musical sound of the rails seemed to perk up our mood and we chatted light-heartedly. I asked Mo more about her family and she revealed a very mysterious past. She refused to say much, and it left a lot of unanswered questions. I would ask her again sometime soon. Once home we were met by my auntie. Her open arms wrapping around us both felt so reassuring. Mo started to cry a little.

'Let us go inside and have some tea'

Auntie was so predictable.

Several days passed and Mo and I stayed about the house helping with the chores: Auntie's leg still troubling her. It was Friday afternoon and Auntie suggested Mo and I should go to the chip shop to save cooking. We arrived at the shop by 4.50 pm and joined the queue as it stretched around the corner. Obviously, everyone else thought a night without cooking was a good idea. At the counter, as our order was given a voice called from the back of the shop.

'Mo, it's me'

Mo looked across the glass cabinet and saw Malcolm filling a potato peeling machine. She turned away and looked out of the shop.

'Mo, it's Malcolm'

I prodded her arm

'Aren't you going to say something?'

'Might do'

Mo shrugged her shoulders.

Malcolm came from behind the counter, calling to the man serving us.

'Be a minute, guv' as he grabbed Mo's arm and led her outside.

'What about the chips?' I called after them.

I did not have any money; it was in Mo's bag.

'Here' Mo threw the bag at me.

'See you outside'

I soon met up with her and she was alone, Malcolm had returned by the back door.

'Quick, let us get home before these get cold'

I wanted to ask what he had said but then I thought if Mo wants to tell me she will.

We shared out the chips and Auntie had cut a whole loaf of bread, thick doorsteps, just like my mum used to. Feeling bloated we just sat around the front parlour for about an hour, not saying much. We had cleared away the newspaper that the chips came in; the smell of them still filled the house. Mo went to the toilet, came back, and sat next to me. Auntie fell asleep curled up in her favourite old chair. It had seen an awfully hard life and was ready for the bonfire. I think she had seen a hard life as well, but I do not think she would appreciate being the bonfire guy. Mo wrapped her legs around me and snuggled up closer.

'I'm bored'

I did not answer her straight away.

'Did you hear me?' she drew back a little and stared at me.

'Yes, I did'

'Well, what's ailing you then?' Mo quizzed.

'Nothing really'

'Well, something's the matter' Mo stood up.

'Don't make a big thing of it' I urged.

Mo was waiting for a reason for my hesitation.

'You know, at the chippie'

'Oh that' she sat down again

'Malc wants to see me tomorrow'

'Well, why didn't you say something on the way home?'

'Don't know really, maybe 'cos I've gone off him'

'But are you going then?

'Oh yes', she smiled.

We left the house at about 10 am the next day and made our way to town. The usual cup of tea and a cake at the cafe set us up. I still wondered whether Jonathon would be there. I liked him a lot and we had not seen each other for long since I lost my virginity to him.

'Over by the fountain' I said excitedly, as the boys came into view.

Mo ran over as I wiped the cake from my mouth. I wish cakes were not so messy or maybe I was just a messy eater. By the time I had caught up to them, Mo had her arm around Jonathon and was whispering in his ear. He seemed to agree with whatever she had said, he smiled at her, and they started to walk away. Mo turned and said

'Come on you two. Beth, grab hold of Malc and follow us'

I was not impressed. This was the second time she had walked off with Jonathon. Malcolm held out his hand and beckoned me to take it. Nervously I did. We walked for some distance away from the centre of town.

'Where are we going?' I asked.

'I think we are going to the warehouses by the river' Malcolm suggested.

'What's there then?

I pressed him for an answer. He smiled at me; the other two turned and smiled as well. I pushed his arm away from me and slowed my pace. He looked upset at this and stopped in his tracks.

'You'll be alright' he assured me.

'No mucking about' I stressed.

'Ok, no mucking about'

We carried on walking. The other two had disappeared ahead of us. We found a seat overlooking the river just by the bridge. I observed the area for ages until Malcolm moved a little closer.

'Did you mean what you said earlier?

'What?

'No mucking about'

I looked at him and realized he wanted more from me.

'Well, yes....and no'

A twinkle came into the corner of his eye.

'It doesn't mean I'm up for it'

'No, I didn't think that, but I would like to kiss you' as he moved even closer.

'I wonder what's keeping the other two?'

I tried to change the subject but getting so close to Malcolm he did not seem so bad. I hadn't really noticed before, probably 'cos he was with Mo. Now though, with Mo getting off with Jonathon, I saw him differently.

'Go on then, just one kiss'

He moved towards me and gently our mouths met. It was a deep kiss and I submitted. I enjoyed it so much that I pulled him into a hug. We continued to kiss like this for ages and eventually came up for air.

'Well, I did say only one kiss'

He gazed into my eyes and replied

'What a kiss!'

I didn't have a lot of experience with that kind of kiss but seemed to take to it very quickly. The other two still hadn't appeared so we lay down on the grass and had sex. Yes, it was good, and I was so pleased that Mo had got off with Jonathon. She didn't realize what a catch Malcolm was. We never saw the other two again that day and eventually made our way back to my auntie's house. After a long goodbye kiss, we agreed to meet up again soon.

# Chapter 5

Three months later, about a week before my 15th birthday Malcolm gave me an eternity ring; only a cheap one, but it meant so much to me. He would have spent more but it was near to Christmas, and he'd splashed out on presents for his family. They were a posh lot and wore their wealth on their sleeve. Everyone in the area thought the father was a member of the mafia as he looked quite Italian in his slim-line suit with a velvet collar and shiny winkle-picker shoes. Apparently, he was from Cardiff in Wales but had spent time abroad during the last world war.

Mo's birthday was 4 days after mine and Auntie thought it would be a good idea if we had just one big party. Mo wasn't sure but could see it would save Auntie baking another cake. Her leg still wasn't right. All of Mo's friends came and enjoyed themselves. Some even had the cheek to borrow my bedroom. I dare not think what they were up to. Feeling giddy and needing to rest a little was the excuse given to Auntie but after the third couple had used the room, I think she cottoned on and blocked any more trips upstairs.

Fruit punch was the drink on offer, but someone laced it with some gin which everyone noticed. Just as well Auntie wasn't drinking. It certainly livened up things and it turned out to be a great night. Jonathon came with Malcolm. They were good mates and as far as I know, never mentioned the swapping of girlfriends. Mind you Mo and I had never referred to it either. Some days afterwards I sat on the sofa with Mo, her legs lying across mine in her usual position.

'Mo' I paused momentarily

'Yes, what is it?'

'Have you had problems with your periods?'

Mo had only started about 6 months ago, quite a late starter.

'Well, yes' replying as she sat up.

'Why do you ask?

33

I hesitated again.

'Well, I missed last month and I'm late this time'

Mo started to give reasons for being late then realized what it could be. She stood up quickly.

'You mean that's two you've missed?'

'Well, yes'

'Goodness Beth, what have you done?'

I looked at her and it dawned on me what she was thinking.

'Maybe I'm pregnant' I sighed.

'No, you can't be'

Mo was distraught at the thought.

'You have been taking care, haven't you?'

'Yes, every time'

'Well, you've got nothing to worry about then'

Mo sat down again and resumed her position lying across my legs.

'You did give me a scare'

We sat and talked about starting a family, now the problem didn't exist. We both agreed we wanted to see something of life before settling down. Mo wanted to go around the world and meet famous people. I, on the other hand only wanted to spend time near the sea. I remembered the happy times when I was younger and before I knew what my dad was really like. He'd make sandcastles with me and sail little paper boats in a pool of water, as the tide rolled in. It only happened a few times but was as clear as though it happened yesterday.

Auntie came into the room and suggested we play cards and as we were both quite bored jumped at the chance.

'What shall we play?' Mo asked

Before an answer was given, she continued.

'Let's play happy families'

'Yes, a grand idea' Auntie quipped as she shuffled the cards.

I looked at Mo and smiled. She obviously had seen the funny side. I didn't feel that easy about things, though. If I wasn't pregnant what could be the answer?

After about an hour Auntie went off to her room and left us to finish another game. Mo had won most of them and was quite high with self-praise. I couldn't celebrate her good fortune as the more I thought of my problem the more I worried. It must have shown on my face as Mo said

'Not still thinking about the phantom baby, are we?'

'Don't be silly' I said, trying to be reassuring to Mo, and myself.

We packed up the cards and went off to our bedrooms. Sleep was not something I wanted though. I needed to know for sure.

On Monday I needed to visit the Doctor to put my mind to rest. Mo took a note to school excusing me for the day. I made an appointment for later the same day at 3 pm.

Upon my return, they were both standing by the open door looking quite concerned.

'How did you get on?' auntie asked

'Well, I....'

My mouth was dry, and I couldn't speak.

'Can I have a drink of water?' I uttered.

Auntie fetched a glass and after taking a mouthful I was ready.

'Well, it's difficult for me to say but the Doctor has confirmed it. Yes Mo, I am pregnant'

Auntie brought her hands up to her face. Mo took my arm and led me into the parlour. Neither of them spoke for quite a while. Finally, Auntie broke the silence.

'What's to be done?'

'Yes, what can we do?' Mo repeated.

Auntie still hadn't gotten over the initial shock and seemed more interested in what the neighbours might say. Mo was supportive and asked if Malcolm knew. I hadn't even thought about him until now.

'Yes, he needs to know' I blurted

'Shall I come with you?' Mo offered

I thought for a moment and then asked Auntie what I should do. Her voice was still strained and continued to sound scornful. Mo led me upstairs to my room for sanctuary. We talked openly now, and it was agreed that I should go alone to Malcolm.

It was almost dark by the time I left the house. Making my way along the cobbled streets, I continued up the hill to the grand gateway that led to Malcolm's house. Leaves littered the driveway and rustled as I kicked them out of my path. The entrance to his house was stately with large white pillars supporting a canopy like the Greek temples I had seen in magazines. I knocked and a smartly dressed woman opened the door. I didn't think it was his mother. I had only seen her once in town when I was with Malcolm, but this person was shorter. She scurried away leaving me on the doorstep. Eventually, the door reopened, and Malcolm appeared

'What are you doing here?' he asked sternly.

'Well, I came to see you'

'My parents don't like me bringing girls to the house'

'Girls, what do you mean, girls?'

He looked sheepish and moved out of the light.

'You know what I mean'

'I'm not sure I do'

'Anyway, what do you want?'

'Well, I came to tell you that I'm pregnant'

He stepped forward and I could see he was not smiling; in fact, he was positively angry.

'It's not mine' he curtly proclaimed

Before I could say another thing, he slammed the door in my face and was gone. I was stunned by his abruptness and stood there for some minutes.

Eventually, I made my way along the path and my walk became faster as I began to cry. I ran most of the way and Auntie's house soon appeared in the gloom. Entering unseen into the house, I rushed upstairs and closed my bedroom door. Sinking into my pillows, my desperate cries were muffled, and I cried myself to sleep.

It must have been about an hour later I heard the door handle turn and Mo came into the room. I sat up and faced her.

'You've been crying'

Mo moved alongside and cuddled me as I began to cry again.

'Did you see Malcolm?'

'Yes'

'Well, why are you crying?'

Before I could reply she moved away a little and grabbed my shoulders. Looking straight into my eyes she could see my pain.

'The bastard, I'll kill him'

I had not seen this side of Mo before and she frightened me.

'He'll be all right when he thinks about it'

I tried to excuse him, but I wasn't convincing, and Mo continued to scorn him. After she had calmed down, we talked, and I realized how this problem had started. Malcolm had wanted to have sex a second time and claimed he didn't need to wear a condom I had gone along with it. Then Mo turned her disdain on me for being so stupid. She blamed herself as when I had first ventured into having sex with the boys, she recalled her promise to look out for me and teach me a thing or two. Either way, it didn't seem to matter now.

As I began to show, Auntie started to spend less and less time with me; preferring to go to Church instead. I can't say I needed her company but what I really wanted was Malcolm to come round. I felt so lonely now and it wasn't helped by Auntie not wanting people to know. I thought maybe I should go and see Malcolm's parents on my own. They were bound to talk to him and make him realize his responsibilities. Mo claimed there was no chance of him wanting the baby if he was pressured by his dad. That would drive him further away. All that was required was patience and he would eventually come to like the idea of being a father himself. I did wait. In fact, I waited for many months and there was no sign from him. I did see his mum again though, out shopping but she didn't acknowledge me and walked straight on. I don't think she remembered me, especially as I now understand Malcolm had quite a few girlfriends. She had probably lost count of the girls whom she'd met.

Auntie had told me from very early on that I wouldn't have the baby at home. She arranged for me to be booked in at a home for girls like me. I didn't know what girls like me were until Mo explained it was an out-of-the-way place where things could happen, and nobody was any of the wiser. In other words, Auntie was ashamed of me and didn't want to upset her neighbours. Going to the Church was her way of dealing with the shame. Personally, I couldn't care less and made a point of walking to town without a coat, to show off my bump. Auntie was old-fashioned and things like this didn't happen to nice girls.

I hadn't gone to school for some time and many of my friends called at the house to see me, but Auntie shunned them and claimed I had something 'catching'. They all knew though; Mo had told them whose baby it was. Malcolm's mother called at the house one day, but I stayed in my room whilst Auntie spoke with her downstairs. I never found out what they spoke about.

# Chapter 6

About 3 weeks before my due date there was a loud knocking at the door. I almost dropped the cup I was washing in the sink. As Mo answered the door, a large figure pushed her aside and went into the parlour.

'Where is she then?'

The voice was easily recognised, and my toes curled up. I gingerly made my way into the room.

'I'm here Dad'

I spoke very softly, almost a whisper. Mo moved in front of me and opened her arms as though to be a shield. My dad looked at me for ages without saying a word. Mo asked him what he wanted, and he stumbled across the room. It was obvious he'd been drinking.

'I wanted to see for myself' he uttered; his manner less threatening.

'Well, it's nice to see you but don't you think you're a little late on the concerned parent bit'

'I know darling, but I've not been well myself'

'Too much drink wouldn't be the reason, would it?' Mo interrupted sarcastically.

He started to explain what happened those years ago with my mum, but again he was cut short by Mo. I know she was trying to be helpful, but I did want to know something of what happened.

'Mo, please make some tea or something' and ushered her into the kitchen.

'Let me look at you' he said as the newspaper he was holding fell from his hand.

Dad seemed to enjoy the sight of my ever-increasing bump. I moved closer and he went to place his hands on me.

'No, not yet'

I was still confused by his presence and needed to adapt to this situation. Mo came back and sat near me. My dad settled in the floral-patterned chair alongside. They were wary of each other and stared all the time. We all sat very quietly until I spoke.

'Why did you come?'

'I just wanted to know you were all right, love'

I hadn't heard that word for ages and it brought back fond memories of my earlier years at home with Mum and David. Yes, David, I hadn't thought of him for ages, and I almost forgot my dad was in the room. With my head clearing I could see that he wanted something and if it was to make amends, then I am not having any of it.

'Well say what's on your mind and then please go'

He didn't speak, picked up his newspaper and left.

Mo closed the door after him and came back into the kitchen where I was finishing the washing up.

'Well, the cheek of it' she snapped and continued to lambaste him.

'Mo, can we not mention him anymore?'

She never replied and started to dry the cups on the draining board. Later, when my auntie came home, we sat at the dining table talking. Nothing was said about my dad calling. Auntie freshened up the pot of tea with hot water and sitting down again asked if there had been any visitors today. Mo started to speak but then looking at me she stopped. My auntie asked Mo what she was about to say.

'My dad called' I interrupted.

I could not let Mo be interrogated.

'Who?' queried Auntie

'My dad'

'Oh, so he kept his word then' she said casually

I was astounded by this and quizzed my auntie further.

'How did you know that he would call?'

'Well, my dear, it's like this'

I sat open-mouthed as she explained that as she was not my legal guardian, he had to be told just in case any decisions needed to be made.

'Well, I don't want to see him, ever again' I shouted and went to my room.

Later, Mo came to my room with excuses for my auntie's actions. I wasn't particularly interested but something auntie said intrigued me. What decisions were they referring to? I thought no more about it and reflected on Mo being there for me. It wasn't the first time she had come to my defence. I recall about two months earlier we had been shopping and a woman in the queue had turned and mumbled something about moral standards. Mo had told her to go away which spurned another comment from the woman about the young not having respect. I thought Mo was going to hit her, but she didn't. Mo was my only consolation at this time, and she had devoted herself to me. I hope it wasn't any feeling of guilt on her part because I never blamed her in any way; it was something that just happened.

At night was when I felt the loneliest and often thought of my mum. Would she have supported me? I wasn't sure, but I hoped she was looking down on me favourably. I hadn't seen the robin for ages and concluded that guardian angels probably didn't exist. Occasionally, when Mo noticed my low spirits she stayed all night, cuddling up to me. She was kind and gentle, aware of my needs. As there was no boy in my life, she played that role. I had been going out with Malcolm for many months previously but never once did I feel like I did with Mo.

When my time was due, I packed a little bag and waited for the taxi. I was still saddened by Auntie's attitude, but she came out to see me off. Mo helped me into the taxi and then leaning in kissed me on the lips. Wiping a tear from her cheek, wished me luck. She was still waving as the taxi turned the corner of the street; Auntie was nowhere to be seen.

The journey was long and very tiring. Eventually, an austere building came into view. I paid the driver and began walking up the worn steps to the entrance. I looked up at the faces looking out through unopened windows. I was struck by the feeling that the prison I had left behind was a holiday camp in comparison to this place. A large woman in uniform met me as I entered the vast hall. I slowed my pace, and she called out

'Come on girl I won't eat you'

Leading me into a room on the right, she pointed to a table

'Put your things down there while we fill out a few forms; let's make it official that you're here'

She moved behind a grand desk and flopped into a brown leather chair that creaked under her weight.

'Now young lady'

Her voice was very stern now

'Your stay here at 'Sunnyhill' will be enjoyable, but it is no picnic, everyone helps around the house doing chores and of course, there are rules to be kept, but more of that tomorrow'

Later, she led me along what seemed to be an endless corridor to the very last door. As I entered, I saw a row of beds lined up along one side of the room. Those nearest the door had a cot at the bed end. Nursing mothers sat looking at me; I smiled and walked to the last bed in the row. Making myself comfortable I returned to greet the others, I hadn't seen anyone for so long and wanted to waste no time in introducing myself. I hadn't said more than a few words when the nurse, who had been so polite so far, vented her anger at one of the heavily pregnant girls. Surely this was not good for her unborn child. The girl, now crying, sat down on her bed, the nurse turned and sounded off at everyone else

'That goes for you lot as well'

'And as for you'

She looked directly at me

'Be ready at 3 o'clock in your dressing gown, the Doctor wants to see you'.

The door had barely closed behind her before a girl passed a comment.

42

'The fucking bitch, I'll get her, I swear I will'.

Strong words, the girl on the bed certainly meant it. I was frightened to ask what it was about.

'Don't worry' a girl standing next to me declared

'It makes us feel better, that's all'.

I smiled and after a short pause, I carried on with my pleasantries; it changed the tone, and everyone made me feel welcome. Later, as I was placing my things into the bedside locker a girl who I now knew as Barbara quipped

'Don't get comfy, you'll be moved up tomorrow'

'What do you mean?'

'Like I say, we play musical chairs, or should I say musical beds in here' she continued

'That's Patsy in the end bed; she goes home tomorrow, so we all move up one'

Totally confused, I spent the remainder of my time chatting to the others. The visit to the Doctor's was uneventful and after supper, I couldn't wait to sleep. Most of the girls sat at the far end talking, I called to them, and they wished me sweet dreams. I had hardly put my head on the pillow when a hand-stretched around the door frame and flicked off the light switch

'Goodnight matron' a chorus rang out sarcastically.

After a sparse breakfast, the matron walked amongst us, singling out certain girls for work. My orders were specified to me with apparent pleasure in her voice.

'The emergency exit steps, use plenty of water and give them a good scrub'

They looked as though they had never been used, so I asked Barbara at lunch

'Why clean them?'

'Everyone does the steps on their first day, don't ask why, it's a mystery to us all'

'You need to work here to pay for your keep'

'There's no charity' another girl interrupted.

Sarah the girl who had slept in the next bed to me last night came over and chatted. We became friends, sharing our thoughts and comparing the size of our very active bumps. Over the next week or so we dreamed about the future; planning how we would celebrate the births. I had made a shawl since becoming pregnant and put my initials in the corner. I told Sarah that my mother had died before she knew I was expecting, and my auntie was ashamed.

'She will spoil your baby rotten; you wait and see'

Yes, I thought, once she saw the child, it would be different.

By now, Sarah and I were up by the new mothers and we each had an empty cot. I think her going into labour set me off as well. The nurse complained it was her night for an early finish and here she was at 5 pm with us two just starting.

My thoughts were no longer with Sarah, I entered unknown territory, my childhood a thing of the past. With a final push, that split me in half, my baby arrived, the pain tempered by the cry of new life. I was exhausted and washed with sweat.

'He's got a good pair of lungs' the nurse declared, wrapping him in a cloth.

Yes, I was right, a boy, I knew it all along. I took him in my arms and pulled the cloth to the side. I melted as my joy overwhelmed me, his little wet and wrinkled face the image of Malcolm. I couldn't wait to show the world this miracle. No one would doubt this was the most beautiful thing that could happen. Soon, I was back in the dormitory and the other girls fussed around like bees. Sarah followed me about 20 minutes later and the attention passed to her. After attending to my son, I fell into a triumphant sleep.

The next three days saw me manage new skills, washing him, changing his nappy, I didn't like that much. Feeding looked so natural as Sarah held her child close to her breasts. I had been taking tablets

44

to dry up my milk as I was told it wasn't suitable; this upset me, as I wanted to bond with my son the natural way. We were now allowed visitors and Mo inspected the new arrival. My auntie showed little interest in picking him up, but I could see her face enjoying the moment. My father surprisingly did pick him up, turning away whilst he kissed and gave a brief cuddle. I think it embarrassed him to let others know how he felt. I had not refused his coming to the home and Mo agreed the past should be forgotten.

'Sign this' my auntie said passing me some papers

'There under your father's signature'

I started to read them, but my auntie insisted

'No just sign them and we can all go home'

The thought of going home and being back with my friends had me signing quickly without question. Malcolm would be amazed at his son's likeness; I do hope he accepts him. My dad then left suggesting a taxi would pick me up later. A woman whom I had seen at home once before came into the room and picked up the papers, I was so excited, only half an hour to go.

'The arrangements are for 3 o'clock, be ready' she ordered.

Back in the dormitory, I prepared everything. My boy looked fine in his new clothes, especially wrapped in the shawl. At exactly the appointed time, the nurse and the woman came into the room. My outstretched arms followed my baby as he was taken from me and whisked out of the room.

'Where are you taking him?' I asked

The nurse who remained at my side assured me

'It will be all right, it won't take long'

She then closed the door and left.

Minutes passed, it seemed forever, and I became anxious. Why were they taking so long? My empty arms yearned to hold him again. Sensing something was very wrong, I rose from the bed and made for the door. A group of people were leaving by the front entrance and turned their heads as I called out.

'Where's my baby?'

A woman huddled a bundle to her breast. It was wrapped in my baby's shawl. I ran towards them, but the nurse came from another doorway and held me back. I tried to struggle free, but another woman helped her. I called out again, screaming but I was powerless in my captor's firm hold. A needle was thrust into my arm; I collapsed to the floor and lost consciousness.

I awoke later, the empty cot beside me. I stood up and went over to Sarah who was sleeping soundly. I shook her hard until she woke up. Startled, she jumped up and made for her own cot, seeing her child was fine turned to me.

'Whatever is the matter?'

'They took my baby'

'That's right; you knew it was like that'

'Like what?' I replied,

'You mean they didn't tell you?'

'Tell me what'

Sarah, taking hold of my shoulders took a deep breath and spoke in a softened tone

'You've given up your child for adoption'

I felt numb. Those papers I'd signed

'No' I murmured

'Please God, no'

My father eventually came back for me and as I stumbled down the old steps, I looked up at the windows that were adorned with many faces when I had arrived. Only one was there now to see me off, her face creased with the pains of labour that consumed her. She mouthed 'good luck' and was gone. I would not miss this place. The journey home to London was uneventful, except that father seemed different to how I recalled him years earlier. He spoke affectionately of my mother and although he never mentioned the violence, I sensed he was remorseful.

Entering my old house, it was as though I had never been away. A time capsule of how it was many years ago. The rickety table, now held together by tape, sat in the front room but no sign of a replacement ashtray. I hadn't seen Father take a cigarette since he'd come back into my life, so I assumed he had given up. An empty bottle of beer stood in the fire grate, so he still had one vice. Mum wouldn't have left it there long; she was so into cleaning the house. Thinking of her saddened me. I found the rest of the downstairs very clean and dust free, as though Mum was still here to tend to him. I didn't linger and went to my old room at the front of the house. Looking out the opened window I couldn't see anybody. A desolate street, unlike how it was when I left that summer's day.

# Chapter 7

The next few months I spent most of my time around the house, having not returned to finish my schooling. It didn't seem important to me anymore and I don't think I would have coped with all the questions. Dad was much improved and spent time chatting with me. He never mentioned mum or the baby ever again, but I did get the feeling he wanted to explain himself. One thing I did notice was he continued to have his chauvinistic side in that I was the head cook and bottle washer; just like mum was.

I managed to get a job on the run-up to Christmas and found this quite a distraction from everything. The shop sold everything possible from candles to jewellery and brooms to buckets. Most food stuff was available but there were many lines permanently out of stock. The owner, Mr. Wallace, was a Polish Jew who made his money during the last war trading in hard-to-find items. My father no doubt would have something to say about that but keep quiet; probably realised my job was important, as the extra income helped at home.

Mr. Wallace was not in good health and quite often was seen collapsed in his office chair. His only time away from the shop was on a Wednesday when he collected his magazine from the newsagents further down the street, as this was one of the few things he didn't sell. I was received well by the other members of staff, and they helped me learn all that was necessary to understand the retail business. I was the youngest employee and made a big impression on all the men who worked in the warehouse behind the shop. The older women who worked in the front tried very hard to keep me under surveillance. I thought of Mo frequently and imagined what she would have been up to with the lads. I did miss her terribly and even Auntie, who I still felt betrayed me. Mo and I did write to each other but some things we couldn't put in the letters just in case anyone else read them. I would have loved to reminisce with her about our times together, feeling the warmth of her silken skin against mine.

One young man called John did make an extra effort to talk to me. From the warehouse door, he would flick little balls of rolled-up silver paper taken from a cigarette packet. He must have made lots of ammunition, as once in range I was bombarded with them. On the last occasion, we were seen by the supervisor and were manhandled towards the office. Passing through the shop she released the grip on my ear and now pushed me from behind. I was so annoyed by this treatment and if we hadn't been in the shop, I would have given an account of myself, I was not a child at school anymore.

After giving her reasons for these actions she left the office, and we were left to expect the worse. The young man was beside himself and tried several times to speak but was told to be quiet. After some minutes of twiddling his pen between his fingers, this short round man with hair parted in the middle spoke

'So, you like each other then?'

We looked at each other and although a smile was trying to show we just dropped our eyes and waited for the next comment.

'I think it's important to have my staff behaving sensibly, don't you agree?' he asked sardonically

Again, we glanced at each other but did not answer. He walked around us and placed his hand upon our shoulders and we both flinched.

'I have an idea' his voice now subdued, almost friendly.

'I have a new shift pattern to set up and I wonder if you two might just be the ones to carry it out'

Understandably I was taken by surprise at this and would have agreed with anything. My mouth was so dry, and I prayed for the ordeal to end.

'You haven't worked in the warehouse yet have you, young lady?'

I had never been called a lady before and still uncertain of his motives, just shook my head.

'I will let you know more in due course' he continued and ushered us out of the office.

'I don't know your name yet' the lad said sheepishly.

I looked at him sternly; I was still annoyed at him for creating this problem.

'My name is Elizabeth, but my friends call me Beth'

He turned to me and chirpily said

'That was lucky in there, Beth'

'I did say, my friends call me Beth'

He did not say anything else, and I walked away.

Over the next few weeks, we carried on this cat and mouse pretence. We knew each other's name but little else. I think I fancied him from the start, but while he played those silly games, I wasn't going to make anything of it.

The end of my 6-month probationary period at work soon came and I was summoned into the office. I wasn't ambitious so I wasn't bothered if my work didn't meet the standard; I could always change jobs. Mr. Wallace was already waiting and closed the door firmly behind me.

'Well,' he said in a warm and positive voice

'How are you getting on?'

'Ok' I muttered

I was surprised he needed to ask, as his spies had obviously been busy watching me.

'I have been hearing some good reports about you'

I smiled reservedly and gave a nervous giggle.

'What's so funny?' he asked

'Nothing sir'

He looked at me for a moment and then said

'Have you done something I should know about?'

'No, definitely not'

'Well, what's got into you then?'

Realising he would not leave it; I offered a lame excuse about something someone had said earlier. He again looked at me, only this time, he laughed

'I know what it is. You were expecting my supervisor's reports to matter to me. Well, they think they are being helpful, but I cannot stand petty goings on'

We both sat down at his enormous desk as he continued to criticize his staff in their absence. I wasn't sure why he should say such things to me, but I remained firmly seated.

'Anyway, enough of what I think. Do you think you could take more responsibility?'

'I'm not sure what you mean'

'Well, we need a new stock controller and from where I'm sitting you are the one for the job. Think you could handle it?'

'Well, I'm not sure'

He did not say anything, and I continued

'I don't think I know enough just yet and what about the other staff; some have been here for ages longer than me?'

'Let me worry about that' he said firmly

'I think we are going to get along famously, but I will expect you to be on top of it'

'Is there any catch?' I asked, still thinking of the worst.

'No dear, no catch, just that I can see your potential and think you deserve a push'

Standing up, he walked around to my side and put his arm around me giving me a bit of a sideways squeeze.

'I was your age when I was given my first real job and from what I can see you could make it as well'

Smiling he continued

'Obviously, your hours will go up to 48, as I would like you to start a little earlier each day to check the paperwork on the overnight delivery'

I was in a state of shock.

'Is that all right then Beth?'

My mouth dropped open.

'Oh, and you can call me Francis, but only when we are in my office, you know people might think something of it'

Still held in his grip I edged away and tried to speak without success.

'Well, that's settled then' as he opened the door for me.

'Yes, thank you, sir, sorry I mean Francis, no sorry I'm not in your office am I'

He just smiled, turned, and closed the door behind him.

Whatever next, I couldn't believe what had just happened.

I made my way back to my job for the day and nobody came to ask what had been said in the office, maybe they already knew but how? I was soon to realise Mr. Wallace had discussed it with another senior member of staff and she had told everyone else. Later that day, I noticed John coming out of the office, a broad smile across his face. I couldn't help but think he had been offered a similar proposition as me. As he passed, I deliberately bumped into him and after saying sorry asked him

'Why the smile?'

'No reason' he quipped as he threw his long golden hair back and walked into the warehouse.

Not happy with his answer and feeling he wanted me to chase him for a reply I followed him.

'Come on tell me or I'll not tell you my news'

'No need, I know your news, in fact, it's your news that made me smile'

'What do you mean?' I said urgently and moved up closer to him.

'Well, you know you've got a new job' then stopped short.

'Don't do this'

I didn't like this tormenting one bit and punched him in his chest with my clenched fist.

'So, you want a fight, do you?'

He came at me and thrust his arms around my small frame. Unable to move, he kissed me on the lips. I did not expect this and obviously being unprepared responded as we both relaxed in each other's arms. Moments later, someone was heard coming into the warehouse. He gently released what little hold he now had over me and stepped away. What was I doing? I kept asking myself this until about an hour had passed, and we came to be alone again.

'What was all that about?' I blurted out in a slightly broken voice.

'Actions speak louder than words' he said as he grinned at me.

I'm sure I blushed. Still not knowing what he was so happy about earlier I pressed him again for an answer.

'Oh that' he sighed reluctantly.

'Well, it's to do with your new job; I am to be your assistant'

It wasn't long before John made another pass at me. Fortunately for both of us, the other workers were now arriving at the clocking-in room. I didn't want to be found kissing as Francis the boss would most definitely take a dim view of it. It could lead to our jobs being on the line.

I gave it some thought and a few days later I asked to see Francis. He obliged and as I sat down in his office, he questioned me about my progress, and I assured him all was going very well. He asked whether something bothered me, and I offered up my reason for being there.

'I think the warehouse could do with a proper audit'

'What do you mean a proper audit?'

He stood up and came around to my side of the large oak desk.

'Well, I am sure that when John and I are checking the stock we get far too many interruptions, and the day staff start taking stock out before we can finalise our counting'

'So' he said and looked at me, waiting for me to speak.

'I was thinking that maybe we should stay late every so often to make sure everything was done properly'

'What a capital idea!'

I was so surprised he liked the idea I quickly continued

'I thought we could start tonight'

'Yes, yes'

He walked back to his seat and looked troubled. After a long pause, he said

'You will need to have a set of keys and the code number for the alarms'

Usually, the cleaner was already there when we arrived in the morning but now, we would be the last ones in the building. Again, he paused then with an assured grin he went to the large rusting safe by the window and took out a bunch of keys, removing several of them. As he handed them to me, I gasped at the thought he trusted me with his business.

'The number of the alarm is my birthday, 3rd May 1915. So, it's 3515'

He asked me to see if John could make it tonight with so little notice. I told him it shouldn't be a problem.

I left and immediately looked around the building for John. I eventually found him standing very close to one of the older women. She seemed to be whispering to him as she leaned forward placing their cheeks together. My news was urgent, so I interrupted them. They broke off and looked startled. The woman turned and slipped out of sight.

'John, can I ask you something?'

'Well, yes' he said slightly bemused.

'Are you free tonight?'

As I waited for his reply it occurred to me that he may think I was asking for a date; I suppose I was. As he was thinking about it, I continued

'The boss wants us to stay late tonight to carry out a full stock check after everyone has gone home'

'Well, I'm not sure'

'We could do it another night if it's a problem'

I was disappointed he didn't jump at the prospect of spending some time with me alone. He had made it obvious he liked me.

'Yes, alright then' his eyes brightening up.

I spent the next hour or so thinking of him and what we might get up to. How far should I take it? Maybe only a kiss. I was so excited. Just before we closed, I saw him with the same woman as earlier, he was arguing with her, but I couldn't make out what they were saying. As I approached, she saw me and said something to him which sounded like 'don't bother then'. She stormed off and never looked back. John turned and calmly asked if I was ready. Yes, I was ready. We locked the side door, picked up our stock sheets and made our way to the far end of the warehouse.

'Well where do you want to start then' he casually asked.

I wasn't sure whether he realised my intentions so replied

'I'll start on this row if you like'

I began marking the boxes off and resigned myself to an evening of boredom and disappointment. He had gone around the corner and said nothing else. About 5 minutes later, I heard lots of banging and shuffling. Thinking he was shifting stock I carried on with my work. Just then I felt warm hands lifting my jumper and gently grasping my small breasts. John pulled me closer and kissed the back of my neck sending a shiver through my body. Without saying a word, he turned and led me to where all the noise came from. He had made a makeshift bed out of packing materials and foam sheets. My heart skipped as I realised, he knew what I was after all along. We lay down and didn't rush things. We spent a long time kissing and fondling each other. Eventually, he removed my jumper and tried to unfasten my skirt. I didn't remember my earlier thoughts on how far we should go and helped him undress me fully. We were now both naked, his bronzed body glistening under the strong overhead lights. It was probably quite cold, but it didn't bother either of us. We spent what seemed ages and he slumped sideways letting out a loud fart.

'That was great' he whispered to me.

'What was, the sex or the fart?'

Nothing further was said for ages as we dressed and had the job of clearing up our nest. I couldn't think of anything to say except maybe thank you but felt it wasn't necessary as he had obviously enjoyed it as well. We did finish the stock check and eventually went home separately.

The next day I clocked in at 7 am as usual only to find John already busy in the staff kitchen. Cups were laid out and the kettle was about to boil.

'Fancy a cupper before we start?'

'Yes please'

This was very cosy, I thought, as he had never made me a hot drink before. The days and weeks that followed were equally pleasant and we often met up, sometimes in his car and occasionally in the park. It was wonderful and I began to think of the future. Unfortunately, John wasn't the settling down kind and over the next 4 years or so, we had an on-off relationship. He had a couple of girlfriends, well older women really and I had a single fling with a lad from the shop next door. He had body odour problems, and I could not relax in his presence, so it didn't last. Mo had stopped writing after she met a man who played the accordion in a band. She went on tour with him and claimed she didn't have time to think about letters. I found this upsetting after we were so close. Mindful that we were grown up now I suppose it was inevitable we would drift apart. It was at my 21st birthday party that

John told me he wanted us to be back together and this time it would be only me in his life. I still doubted his word but allowed him to make love to me after most of the guests had gone home. I was desperate for this and in my haste, I forgot that I no longer took the birth pill. He wasn't concerned either, when during sex I pointed out that we were not taking precautions. He was inside me and hesitated for a moment. Then, without saying anything carried on. It was good to be with a warm body again and I enjoyed every moment of it.

We carried on seeing each other and it wasn't until the beginning of March that I realized I was expecting his child. I had never told him about my past and even though I seemed to be repeating previous mistakes I knew this time it was to have a happy ending. We agreed not to get married until after the baby was born, as the bump would make me look fat in the photos. We did set up a home together and when I had to give up work; Francis gave John a supervisor's job and a pay rise, so we managed quite well. During the last weeks of my confinement, John spent extra time working as much overtime as he could. He was so attentive to my ever-growing size and felt our baby move every time he passed by me.

Soon the day arrived, and we were blessed with a tiny little girl whom we named Charlotte. This couldn't be more different to my last baby's arrival and those awful people who took him away. I didn't imagine this day would ever happen, so I was full of the joys of motherhood. I ventured out at least once a week to get basic shopping but left the main shop to John who always brought back something special for me. Flowers seemed to be a favourite and our living room was decked out with seasonal blooms on almost every surface, even in the bedroom there were pot plants. The colours were amazing, and I felt a little guilty for not buying him something. I managed to contact Mo and wrote many letters and she promised to visit but for some reason, she never came. I did so look forward to seeing her face when she saw my little Charlotte.

Time passes slowly when you're at home most of the time, but my new baby always kept me busy. She bonded very well with John and her eyes lit up each time he peered into the cot as she lay gurgling. The weather had prevented me from arranging to visit John at work, being so wet and cold. So, it was a welcome change when the sun came out and appeared to want to hang on in there for the rest of the day. It would be nice to surprise John and call the shop.

Dressing Charlotte in a beautiful outfit I had made, I recalled the shawl I had made for my first born but this upset me so without further hesitation we made our way to see John. Entering the shop, I was met by Janet the store cleaner.

'What a bonny little boy'

I looked at her in dismay and she continued

'John has been telling us all that you and your son have been doing well'

'But it's a girl, her name is Charlotte'

Janet picked up her bucket and tried to apologise. I knew that John had wanted a boy, but this really shook me. By now several members of the staff had surrounded us and were cooing at her tiny size and beauty. John appeared at the doorway to the office and called out.

'You lot get back to work, there will be plenty of time to see the baby'

I was ushered away with his hand pressing into my back.

'What are you doing here?' he demanded.

I had only heard that tone of voice once before when he accused me of wasting money on baby clothes.

'I thought it would be nice for you to see Charlotte and me'

'Well maybe next time you'll let me know when you're going to spring surprises'

He still seemed annoyed at my arrival at the store, so I went to the door, turning I said

'I know when I'm not welcome, so your baby, Charlotte that is, will see you at home tonight'

He didn't reply but just closed the door behind me. Making my way to the exit I overheard several of the staff talking aloud.

'The bastard needs his balls cut off' said one woman

'Such a beautiful baby as well' they were nodding at each other.

I didn't linger and set off for home as the store faded behind me a teardrop rolled down my cheeks. What were they saying and what made John so mad? At home, Charlotte was fed and cleaned up before she was laid to sleep. John was late home again, but I said nothing to him as he still had a frightening face on him. Several months passed and his timekeeping got worse, and I concluded that he was seeing someone else, probably at the store. He led a secretive life and expected me not to notice. Things like doing his own washing in the twin tub and locking the bathroom door when having a shower. Probably had lipstick on his clothes or scratch marks down his back that he thought would give his game away, but I knew.

The flowers had stopped ages ago, but I found a receipt in his top pocket dated only last week for a dozen roses. It wasn't my birthday or any other memorable event so this was the last straw. I had to confront him with my suspicions. Later that night he came in a little worse for wear, he'd obviously been drinking. After his meal was eaten, he started to watch television in the living room. I stood in front of the screen and ask him outright.

'Are you seeing another woman?'

'Get out of the way' he shouted as he swung his arm at me

'I'm trying to watch this'

I didn't move except to turn and switch off the set.

'Do I get an answer?' I wasn't letting him ignore me.

'Yes, yes I am'

I froze at the realisation of it being true.

'Now can you move; I want to watch this program'

I did move but let him switch it on himself. Putting on the kettle in the kitchen I proceeded to make myself a cup of tea. I'd never made one without asking if he wanted a drink but now, he seemed so distant as though he was no longer there. Although we shared the marital bed, we never had sex, not even a goodnight kiss. It was like living with a stranger; even our daughter seemed to cry when he picked her up. Maybe she sensed he was an outright bastard. I later found out he had a son with another woman from work. After almost a year he just picked up his stuff and left. I don't know where he went and couldn't care less so I didn't ask.

# Chapter 8

John had some redeeming features as he never emptied our joint bank account when he left. I stayed at the house, but the rent and food costs were so high it was obvious I needed to move, so gave my notice. Looking at the property adverts in the local shop window for something cheaper I came across a small cottage for sale in the same village as Mo. It looked ideal but wasn't sure whether I could get a mortgage as I wasn't working. I still took down the details and keep thinking about it throughout the rest of the day. After having a light meal, my appetite had gone since he had left, I set about trying to write a letter to Mo. Eventually, I placed the crumpled sheet sprinkled with perfume into an envelope. I had thrown it away just after starting to write as I didn't know what to say. Then realised it was my last sheet so recovered it from the bin. I didn't say much about John except he was gone for good, and I missed her terribly.

Charlotte was very active now and I wanted Mo to see her as she made progress so invited her to stay before I moved. Almost by return, I received a reply. It was a short letter and told me to expect her in the next few days. I was so pleased and prepared the house for a most welcome guest. I wasn't sure how we would be together after so long so made up the spare room, the love we had shared was a distant memory.

Three days later a taxi pulled up outside. I grabbed Charlotte and made my way to the gate.

'Hi there' she called out as money was thrust into the driver's hand.

He didn't get out to help with her bags, so she asked for her tip back. He grunted and pulled away almost knocking her down.

'What a nasty man Charlotte' turning her away from his departing car.

'Mo, it's so good to see you again'

We brushed our cheeks together and as she was barely through the front door Charlotte was snatched from my grasp and cuddled by Mo.

'She's gorgeous, just like her mum'

I collected the bags and closed the door. Placing them at the foot of the stairs I showed Mo the way into the living room.

'Now what drink would you like?'

'Well, a long drink would probably be better but have you something stronger; that was the worst journey I have ever been on?'

I could see she was quite exhausted from the trip. Taking Charlotte from her I placed her in her cot by the window.

'I'll see what I've got to drink'

A bottle of brandy was kept in John's cupboard, well my cupboard now so I think we can use it.

'So, what have you been up to?' Mo enquired.

'Well, nothing really'

'Don't tell me I've come all this way and all you can say is nothing really' and continued

'It sounded like you were about to top yourself in the letter'

'Sorry I didn't mean to frighten you, but I was feeling low at the time, but now you are here'

'Yes, I'm here and after you've poured the drink you can sit down and tell me everything'

After a while, Charlotte started making a lot of noise and as this was the time for her evening wash. I excused myself and set off up the stairs. Mo wasn't having any of that and soon took over in the bathroom. As Mo washed Charlotte's hair, she commented on how she wished things were different; that she could have children. After drying, Charlotte was laid in her cot and speaking in a soft voice Mo settled her down without a fuss. Something I hadn't always managed. Without disturbing her we slipped downstairs and opened a bottle of wine. I explained about giving notice on the house and Mo suggested Charlotte and I could stay with her while I made other arrangements.

'Let me propose a toast' Mo raising her glass.

'Yes, lets'

'What shall we say?' Mo was stuck for the right thing to say.

'To us' raising my own glass.

'And Charlotte'

'Of course, yes my Charlotte'

Mo sat down opposite me and with piercing blue eyes looked at me.

'Now you can tell me what's going on in that head of yours'

Her determined approach made it very difficult to not answer her.

'Well, I don't know where to begin' I said cautiously

'Well, you can start with that husband of yours, 'ex' should I say'

I hadn't written to Mo much during the last year, so I really needed to fill her in with some of the history, so she understood why I was so paranoid during those early days.

'I think it all started before I married him when he furtively spent time with other girls at work. Then, after I became pregnant and stayed at home it must have got out of hand'

'The bastard' Mo interrupted

'Sorry, carry on'

I did so and once everything that happened was relayed, I poured myself and Mo another drink.

'There's nothing left to save then?' asked Mo

I think she knew the answer to that, and I didn't waste a reply just looked at her and raised my eyebrows.

Later, after Mo had told me her news we sat down together on the settee and had a little cuddle. Nothing more as all we wanted was comfort.

'I'm sure you will find something you can afford' Mo suggested

'Oh, I have this cottage in mind, and I'd love to see it'

'What cottage?' quizzed Mo

'It's one that I saw in the window of an agent in town'

'Where is it?' Mo edged up onto the seat arm and leaned forward excitedly

'Well, it's not actually for rent, it's for sale'

Mo stood up and picked up the bottle off the cupboard top and poured the remainder of the wine into her glass.

'How are you going to buy?'

'I was hoping to get a mortgage; I don't see that being a problem, lots of people get them'

'You realize you're not working and have no deposit' Mo said sternly

I didn't reply and just looked blank as I hadn't really thought about it.

'Show me the details then'

I couldn't as I only had the address and a contact number for the agent.

'We will have a look at it tomorrow' Mo suggested

'I'm afraid that may not be possible as it isn't in this town'

'Well, where the hell is it?' Mo asked expectantly

'You will be pleased to know it's in your village down by the Wharf'

'You mean Lighterman's Wharf down by the canal?'

'Yes, it's the old cottage set back amongst the trees, high on the bank of the canal'

Mo didn't say a word and slowly sat close to me.

'Darling, you mustn't dream; things like that don't happen that easily'

'I know but it is still worth a visit, don't you think?' I said eagerly

'Possibly, my dear, we'll see what tomorrow brings'

My mother would say that when things were tough and things always turned out all right, so I still felt good about the whole thing.

The following day we spent walking around my town and Mo commented on how quaint it was. I wouldn't have said quaint, more like the old world. The buildings were dirty and the pavements untidy, but they gave out a warm feeling. Many of them dated back to the last century and were very ornate with faces cut into the stonework. Some had large window edges that the pigeons had taken up as their roost;

their mess had eaten into the stone and left it disfigured. We stopped at the café on the main road and reminisced about our time together chatting up the boys.

'I think I was a bit naive then' I said with a sigh

'I wasn't' Mo retorted

'Well, I did learn a lot, but that's now in the past'

'About this cottage then' Mo changed the subject

'I have to be back by next Friday, so that's three days away, so if you can get yourself organised, we can travel back together'

'Yes, I think so' I said without really thinking.

The next day we busied ourselves packing and arranged for almost everything to go into storage. When Friday arrived, we locked up the house and climbed into the waiting taxi.

'Thank goodness it's not that awful man who brought you last week, Mo'

'Yes, I wouldn't want him to have shown his face again'

It would be a long journey, so Charlotte had already had a long nap before we left, hopefully avoiding her getting miserable. My dreams of a new chapter of my life gave me a feeling of excitement and I had butterflies in my tummy. The clouds were closing in, and it was getting dark as we pulled up outside Mo's place and no time was lost getting inside. Charlotte had slept most of the way but woke up just as we put the luggage in the hallway. The house was cold, and the strange surroundings obviously upset her. A crying session lasted for a good 5 minutes. She stopped as the kettle boiled, and we all sat down for a well-deserved cup of tea.

'Sorry I haven't got any cake; I wasn't expecting you to return with me'

'That's not a problem; it's so good to be here'

Having finished the second cup of tea, I proceeded to sort out my luggage. To my surprise I realised

'There's only one bedroom'

Mo and I hadn't spent any time together like we used to while she was at my house, using the spare bedroom throughout her stay. It was never mentioned that we were once lovers. Mo realised what I was about to say when I came back.

'I can sleep on the settee if you like?' Mo said in a soft voice but looking disappointed.

Without hesitation, I suggested that we would share the bed, small though it was. Mo said nothing and prepared a pile of sandwiches. She did find a packet of jam tarts she didn't know she had hidden at the back of the cupboard.

'Not sure how long they have been there, they should taste all right' Mo selling them to me.

I put Charlotte to bed and after a long soak in the bath, tucked myself up in bed. Mo was still in the bath, and I must have fallen asleep. I awoke with a start as she climbed in beside me. I wasn't used to anyone being in my bed as John hadn't been there for so long. With some apprehension, we moved closer and cuddled for what seemed ages. What would I do if Mo wanted to get it on with me? I didn't answer my own question, as Mo kissed me on the forehead.

'Goodnight darling' she sounded very tired and now must admit I felt a little disappointed.

'Goodnight, see you in the morning'

I had an answer to my question now but turning slightly I kissed her lightly on the lips. Mo responded and that night we felt each other as though time had not moved from when we shared a bed in her mother's house.

The next day was Saturday, and the agents were only open until 12 o'clock, so we hurried off after breakfast to have a look at the cottage.

'Truly amazing, I don't think I've seen anything so beautiful in all my life' Mo exclaimed as we turned the corner.

A strange feeling washed over me, and I felt attracted to the little cottage, now well-overgrown with ivy and weeds scattered amongst the flowers. It was obvious that nobody had lived here for a long while. We needed no invitation to explore the grounds and venture up to the front door. Mo kept sighing and mumbling

'What a find'

I, on the other hand, started to feel insecure and a thought ran through my mind that beautiful as it was, it was beyond my reach.

'Come on, let us go' I called out to Mo and lifted Charlotte up into my arms.

She was able to walk with some support but couldn't cope with the uneven ground around her. Charlotte tried to resist and wanted to be put down again, but I was now walking towards the gate if you can call it a gate. Hanging by a broken hinge it was in dire need of repair. Mo didn't speak as we made our way back to civilisation. At Mo's flat the usual routine of putting on the kettle took place and whilst the water rose in temperature Mo finally spoke.

'Pity it's not for rent'

I didn't answer just looked at Charlotte who was digging in the cupboard. Cereals and tins were kept there, and she must have seen them when the door was open. With some difficulty, I pulled her away offering a bar of chocolate as a bribe.

'Yes, it would be nice if it was for rent, but all that work'

'I know but I could help you'

'Bit of a moot point though, as it isn't for rent'

We drank our freshly made tea and Charlotte ate her chocolate, well some of it, as the rest was around her mouth and on the arm of the chair.

'Look, I think it's worth ringing the agent and seeing if it could be rented' Mo said optimistically

'Do you think so?'

My thoughts raced at the prospect.

'What's the time' Mo said grabbing the telephone from behind the curtain. It had been pushed there because little hands were playing with it.

'Where's the number?'

'Here'

I wasn't sure whether I wanted to know but let her proceed with the call.

'Hello, yes, it's about the cottage you have for sale down on the wharf. Is it still available?'

'He must have said yes as Mo continued to ask questions about the person selling it.

'We are seriously interested in renting it' she went on.

Her expression dropped to one of sadness as he spoke but soon, she was smiling and thanking him.

'Ok, so you'll let me know then?'

Placing the handset down Mo said

'Keep your fingers crossed'

'Tell me, tell me what he said?'

I had urgency in my voice.

'This calls for another cup of tea'

Mo was elusive

'So, what did he say?'

I needed to know, and Mo seemed to delight in delaying the answer.

'He is going to ask Mr. Wallace to consider your proposition'

'Mr Wallace' I quickly queried.

'Yes, he told me the guy's name without realising and quickly backtracked calling him his client'

I couldn't but hope it was the same Mr. Wallace who had insisted I call him Francis. No call came before 12 o'clock so we settled down for the weekend not knowing the outcome.

About 3 pm on Sunday a call did come through from a man who didn't introduce himself, only said if I wanted to talk about the cottage, I was to meet him there at 6 pm that day.

'Mo, you'll have to look after her for me, please'

Mo tried to dissuade me from going alone but Charlotte had only just gone down for her afternoon sleep, so I hastily got changed and made my way there. I arrived a few minutes early and found nobody around. It was ages before a large black car pulled up at the bottom of the hill. A man in uniform stepped out and walked up to the cottage and requested I talk to the man in the car.

Nervously I arrived at the car. A hand opened the door, and a croaky voice asked me to get in. I wasn't in the habit of getting into strange cars with strange men, so with some trepidation, I did. It was getting dark by now and this all seemed unreal. I couldn't make out whom I was speaking to and asked

'Is there a light in here?'

'Of course, my dear' came a voice I recognised.

'Hello, yes that's better' he continued.

'Well, I never, it's young Beth' he exclaimed.

My surprise was obvious as I began to giggle.

'I'm so pleased it's you, Mr Wallace, Francis I mean'

'What a coincidence, my word you do look well' he commented and opened a small cupboard in front of him.

'Would you like a little tipple?' waving a flask at me.

'No, not for me'

'Yes, I do drink too much, but what the hell, you only live once'

These words rang true but so far there had not been many occasions that fitted my life, which warranted a celebratory drink.

'Now then you're probably wondering why the urgency to meet'

'Well, yes'

'I am going abroad on Tuesday and it's unlikely I will return for some time' he explained

'But I understand you like the cottage?'

'Yes, but I haven't any money right now'

'Umm...., so you have no money but you like the cottage'

'Yes'

'Don't worry about that right now, let's talk about you? Where's that husband of yours?'

My eyes dropped and he didn't wait for an answer.

'Well then, what about you?'

After several more personal and rather private questions he made a proposal that if I could assure him that I wasn't just wasting his time then he would consider renting it out to me. He would let me know by 12 o'clock Monday and I was to stay by the phone. Mo was waiting for me when I got back to her place and insisted, I fill her in. My thoughts were with Charlotte and once I saw her still sleeping, I gave over all that had transpired with Mr. Wallace.

'Well, that sounds promising' Mo said encouragingly.

I wasn't sure whether it would be rented out; I still found the whole thing so unreal.

'I hope so' I said reservedly.

'God you are so negative' Mo shouted at me almost waking Charlotte.

'I'm sorry but you are' she continued as she went to the tabletop with the drinks on.

'Well, I think it calls for a toast'

Pouring two glasses of wine she turned and raised her glass as she handed me the other.

'Here's to a good result'

She wasn't going to let me ponder the thought of not getting the cottage so spent the rest of the day talking about how we would clear up the garden.

'Goodness knows what we will find under all that growth' she speculated.

Monday came and we all arose to a bright and fine morning. The sun made an appearance and started to rise into the few clouds that had lingered after yesterday's dismal afternoon. Charlotte had slept through without stirring. Mo and I took advantage, not getting out of bed except to use the toilet, and then returning to have another cuddle. We didn't have sex every night and cuddles became the main comfort for us both. Our initial needs were now met, and we felt so secure just being together.

'I suppose we ought to get up soon' Mo said giving a long yawn.

'Must we?'

With that, she was out of bed and wrestling with her dressing gown, the arms not being where they were last night.

'Sorry, that's my fault, I wore it to go to the loo'

'You could have put the sleeves back instead of inside out'

Mo was a little displeased but still offered to make me a cup of tea in bed. This I gladly accepted and curled up under the blanket. Moments later she appeared next to me without the tea.

'We've had a power cut so the tea will have to wait'

My mouth was dry so we both went into the kitchen seeking out the orange juice made last night for Charlotte.

'Don't you feel guilty, drinking the baby's juice?

'No, there's a full bottle made up in the fridge, there'll be enough for us all'

Pouring it into the cups we both sipped it together.

'That's revolting' Mo screamed.

'My drinks are not too bad'

The drink was warm and almost undrinkable, but with my thirst needing to be quenched, I drank mine. Mo set hers down on the worktop and went into the lounge, seeking out the telephone.

'God knows how long the power has been off, where's the number for the electric company?'

She was rummaging through the papers on the mantle only to find the gas bill.

'Fat lot of good that will be'

She was annoyed now and tossed the papers across the room. I had not seen this side of her before so after she calmed a little, I offered to help.

'Try directory enquiries'

Dialling the number and finally getting through to the right department she was advised the power would be off for most of the day, a major fire in the town had burnt through the cables. Resigned to the problem that neither of us could avoid we settled down to breakfast. The milkman coming early saved us from the warm milk from the now useless fridge. The morning was difficult and the usual chores like cleaning and washing didn't get done. Neither of us showered and cleaning up Charlotte wasn't very pleasant without hot water. Lunchtime was fast approaching, and the expected telephone call hadn't arrived.

'I don't think I'm going to get the cottage, Mo'

'Give over; you're just being your usual pessimistic self'

Mo was still agitated since first thing, and I couldn't quite understand why.

'Are you all right Mo?'

'Nothings the matter' she snapped.

'Yes, there is, I can tell'

'Well, if you must know it's the cottage'

'What do you mean the cottage?'

'You're going to hate me for saying this, but I hope you don't get it'

I was so taken by surprise I stumbled backwards into the armchair.

'How could you' my voice broke up.

Mo didn't continue and all I could do was speculate what had brought about this bout of anger.

'Would you like to explain?'

Mo looked at me, her eyes filling with tears. Now crying, she came over and threw her arms around me.

'I'm sorry'

'Why?'

Mo released her grip and drawing my face towards her, she kissed me hard on the lips. I was even more confused now and I pushed her away. My mind raced and I just couldn't understand.

'Please tell me what it is?' I urged.

'I don't want you to leave me, ever, I mean never'

I came quickly to my senses and realised she feared that our relationship would end if I moved out. I thought about this many times in the last few days and it was obvious that Mo had been thinking the same.

'Don't be silly'

'But I love you'

Mo had never actually said this before and it was quite unexpected to hear, although I think I knew all along.

'Darling, I love you too and I'm not going to let my moving split us up'

Mo seemed reassured by this and offered to make us a cup of tea.

'Bugger it' Mo shouted from the kitchen.

'I know, the powers are still off'

We did laugh and after a reassuring cuddle and our eyes wiped with tissues it was decided to ring the agents. It was about 12 o'clock and the phone kept ringing out but with no reply. Strange I thought; surely there would be someone to answer the phone. This setback wasn't going to upset me and upon my suggestion to have lunch in town, we all set off as soon as Charlotte was dressed. Arriving by the town hall we looked across towards the agent's shop.

'My god, look at the state of that!'

Mo pointed along the road towards the open-air swimming pool. There must have been at least 5 fire engines and miles of hosepipe strewn everywhere like a spider's web.

'Let us go and see what's happened' Mo said excitedly.

'No' I cautiously replied.

'I've got Charlotte to think of'

'Well, I'm going to get closer, you wait here a moment'

And with that Mo darted along the wet pavement towards the engines. She was gone for what seemed ages and eventually came scurrying back.

'Do you want the good news or the bad?' she taunted.

'Don't mess around, what's going on?'

'Well, the agent's shop is still standing but there's no one there, been evacuated by the fireman' she said, still catching her breath.

'What shall we do now then?'

It seemed all hope was lost, how would Mr. Wallace contact me now. If I didn't get his message today, he would be long gone by tomorrow. Just then a hand tugged the shoulder of Mo.

'Maureen Thompson is that you?' a man dressed in a long jacket asked.

Not sure whether to reply Mo stood back and with a degree of reluctance said.

'Yes, do I know you?'

'Yes, you probably don't remember me now, but we used to be neighbours when you lived in Saxon Street with your parents'

'Goodness, your name is' Mo hesitated and then

'Jason, Jason that's it, isn't it?'

'I work for Jackson and Co the agents; you spoke to me the other day about the cottage'

'Yes, the cottage' I interrupted.

'Tell me about the cottage, has Mr. Wallace been in touch?'

'Yes, that's what I'm trying to tell you both. He sent word that you can have the cottage, but our phones were not working so we couldn't let you know'

Mo looked at me and I looked at Charlotte. Nothing could have been sweeter to my ears at that point. Mo picked up Charlotte and I wrapped my arms around them both. Turning, I then grabbed the young man and kissed him on the forehead. His embarrassment was revealed in his bright red cheeks. Mo seemed to be as happy about the news, being reassured by our declaration of devotion earlier.

'There is a mountain of papers back at the office to sign, but they will have to wait until we get the all-clear from the fireman' Jason said bringing us down to earth.

Eventually everything was arranged, and I agreed to move in as soon as possible. Finally, my life was improving; no man to get in the way. Charlotte and my dearest Mo are at my side. Clearing up the garden was a challenge but with the help of our newly acquired friend and neighbour Jason, it soon had some shape and order. Charlotte lost no time exploring the open space; fortunately, all the fences were intact leaving just the gate to repair. I felt at home the minute I carried my bags up the path those weeks before. The inside was not too bad, a little old-fashioned but what the hell; it was a lot better than I had ever imagined I could achieve. My priority now was how to pay the rent. Unfortunately, funds were getting low so going back to work seemed the only option. I checked out the local vacancies and picked out something that fitted in with Mo who offered to help with childminding. Jason even did some as well. Things couldn't be better, and we all settled down to this idyllic life. Mo and I had continued to be lovers and although she only lived a short walk away often stayed overnight.

Several months passed and I held a small party for the neighbours and friends. Mo and Jason came together. She had picked him up; his car being fished out of the river a week earlier following an accident when he skidded and left the road. It was a resounding success and as the evening progressed, I lost sight of Mo. I searched the kitchen and looked outside but couldn't find her. I asked Charlotte who was now nearly 20 months

'Where is Mo?'

She didn't say anything but started to climb the stairs. I picked her up and made my way upstairs. She wasn't in the toilet, so opening my bedroom door I wasn't expecting to find Jason with his trousers around his ankles lying next to Mo. I quickly closed the door before either of them noticed me. Charlotte had been held in my arms facing backwards so hadn't seen what Mo was up to; thank goodness.

I never said anything to Mo or Jason about what I had seen but it didn't seem right that they should deceive me. My relationship with Mo never seemed the same again. She still came to my bed, and we still enjoyed every moment, but it always bugged me that she was obviously seeing us both. I needed her and was reluctantly prepared to share her. They still helped with the childminding and to my knowledge didn't do anything when Charlotte was awake. Well, I hope they didn't.

# Chapter 9

It must have been on my first anniversary of moving to the cottage that I received some very upsetting news. A letter arrived saying Mr. Wallace had died in a plane crash some weeks earlier and my rent was to be paid as normal by the solicitor instructed to take over his affairs. I heard nothing for some time and started looking at the adverts for accommodation nearby just in case. My heart wasn't in this and even when asking for details I felt I was betraying Charlotte by not letting her grow up in this paradise.

One day I received a telephone call from a solicitor by the name of Mr. Peabody who asked me to attend the reading of Mr. Wallace's will. He suggested it would be of interest to me. So, I arranged for Mo to look after Charlotte and caught a taxi to their offices as they were not easy to find. A long statement was read out by the solicitor and all those assembled were beginning to get either frustrated if they thought they were beneficiaries or bored if they didn't. If like me there was little interest. Of course, there was the issue of whether the new owner would put up the rent or even worse sell from under me. I did have a good tenancy agreement, but you never know what might happen. Standing up, Peabody leaned across the table and poured a glass of water.

'Get on with it' was heard quite clearly from the back of the room, but nobody seemed to know who said it. Looking over the top of his spectacles he proceeded to read the will. Coming to the bit about Mr. Wallace's property he again looked up at the now very silent group. Several houses and apartments were mentioned, and they were to be sold and the proceeds mostly went to charities. My heart was sinking rapidly, and I began to fear the worst. Then, like a bolt of lightning the cottage was mentioned and my name. I missed what was said and stood up

'Sorry can you say that bit again, please' my voice broke.

Everyone turned and frowned at me. They were waiting for their interests to be read out and didn't want any interruptions.

'It is most irregular to ask questions, least of all during the reading,' said Peabody.

'Tell her again and let's get on with it' rang out from the anonymous voice at the back.

Coughing to clear his throat, Peabody continued

'And the property known as Rose cottage situated at Church Road, in the village of Oare, near Faversham in the county of Kent shall be left in its entirety to the current occupier Ms. Elizabeth Yates'

I'm no legal wizard but that sounded like he's left the cottage to me. After the reading had finished and most of the people had left, some shouting

'Tight bastard never left me a bean'

'Did you ever hear such a thing, leaving his warehouse and shops to the staff'

There didn't seem to be many attendees who praised or celebrated his life or his passing. I approached Peabody and made myself known to him.

'Ah yes, the little lady, wait there for a moment until we close the outer doors'

With that, he went off into another room. I sat in the large armchair he had previously occupied and contemplated the news that for some obscure reason Mr. Wallace, Francis, had favoured Charlotte and me. Upon his return Peabody and his assistant ushered me into his private office.

'Well, my dear, what do you make of it then?'

His assistant sat close by and nodded like a demented parrot.

'I'm sure I don't know' I replied nervously

'Well, he certainly liked you'

Passing me a letter I read it quickly. Shaking a little, I passed it back to him. It was addressed to the solicitor and explained why he had written his will in the manner outlined.

'There's lots of paperwork to complete so you will be contacted as soon as the property can be transferred to your name, maybe 4 to 6 weeks'

Still shaking I thanked him and asked if a taxi could be called. The journey was slow as the traffic seemed to come from out of nowhere. Eventually, I was back at the cottage and was met along the path by Charlotte running towards me. I lifted her up and held her close kissing her beautiful head of hair as she twisted and looked back towards the cottage. Mo stood smiling at us but did not speak. As I entered the front door, I could hear the kettle boil so without any delay my coat was thrown at the hook, missing by a mile and I proceeded to make a drink.

'Well then?' asked Mo who was now very intrigued why I had such a large smile.

'Let's take the drinks through into the living room first'

Mo was itching to find out what had happened, so I started by explaining what Peabody had told us. About the mild-mannered man who had suffered great hardship when arriving in England as a refugee from Poland in 1938.

'What's this got to do with the cottage, are you being thrown out or not?' she interrupted.

'Wait and see; I'm trying to explain'

I couldn't keep up the torment for long and quickly explained how Francis left his family behind, later to be told they had all perished at the hands of the Germans when their town was attacked. Apparently, he had no living relatives to pass on his estate and as I had been so like his own wife and Charlotte resembling his firstborn daughter Meira, he felt it appropriate to settle something on us in memory of his loved ones.

'Bloody good show, so he's left you the cottage' Mo exclaimed loudly

'No, it's not like that Mo'

'Well, I think he's brilliant, whatever his reasons'

Taking my cup back to the kitchen I wondered why Francis never mentioned his family before, maybe it was painful. Mo was now playing with Charlotte on the floor and appeared so full of joy. I felt very subdued and went out into the garden and began picking the dead heads off the roses. Although this news had come as a welcome surprise, my thoughts were solely with Francis. I made a promise to myself to remember his name in some way through the cottage and gardens. Maybe a plaque on the wall, or a small memorial by the oak tree overlooking the canal. I would give it some thought and decide later.

In the next few weeks, I dwelled on the letter that Peabody had let me read at the will reading. It was how I came to learn about his desire to honour his lost family. I thought this would be an obvious choice to commemorate his life if I could keep the letter within the walls of the cottage. So, when Peabody came to see me with the papers I asked for the letter and without hesitation he took it from his briefcase and handed it to me.

'I was going to ask if you would like it'

'Yes, I have a special reason to keep it'

After Peabody had gone, I secreted it in my bedroom and didn't tell Mo. This was something I needed to think about without her usual bullish approach. Now the cottage was officially mine I rang Mo on the telephone and asked her to have tea with Charlotte and me. During the evening I asked Mo how she was coping with living in her place. In a subdued voice, she explained

'All the rooms need a lick of paint, and the landlord says I have to do it myself; he's a right shit'

'What if you had the chance to move?'

'Yes, if there was half a chance' she replied.

'Well maybe you would like to move in here, with me'

Mo looked at me with bright blue eyes that shone as tears began to flow.

'Beth, I love you so much'

Some weeks later after settling her arrears with her landlord, she hired a small van or so I thought at the time. Apparently, an old boyfriend had lent it. After she moved in, we became closer and her confusion over whether she wanted male company or mine was never in question. Many years passed and Charlotte did well at school and developed into a beautiful young woman. She had many friends and was rarely at home. This left me with lots of free time as Mo worked all week in the town. We had decided that she would be the breadwinner and I could play the doting housewife. The area we lived in hadn't changed much over the years and I found many places to visit and enjoy. I loved walking along the canal towpath and imagined the horses that previously worked there dragging lighters laden with coal and grain. I particularly liked the wildflowers that made an appearance early in the spring but were soon lost as the banks were soon overgrown with tall grass and stinging nettles for the rest of the year. Charlotte liked it here as well and we spent many hours playing hide and seek behind the many shady trees and bushes.

Now though, she had more distractions, and the young men were drawn to her like bees to nectar. I tried to remember how it was back when I was her age, but the hurt was hard to bear. She wasn't going to suffer as I did. At the earliest opportunity I had given her all the information a girl should have to avoid mistakes and I think it worked as she kept telling the boys to 'sod off' when they came around. Especially when they said something about Mo and me living together. Personally, I couldn't care what they thought but I did worry about Charlotte. One evening when we were sitting around the table picking at our food, Mo asked Charlotte what she was going to do when college finished in a few weeks' time. Charlotte had already been thinking about it and had attended an interview without telling us. I was so proud of her and wondered where the baby girl I'd nursed all those years ago had gone. Eighteen years had flown by. The job was offered to her, and she duly started.

It was about two months later that she came home all excited and tripped over the step as she entered the house.

'Careful' I remarked

'What's the rush?'

'I'm so happy mum'

'Don't tell me, you've been given a pay rise' I quipped

'No, better than that'

I felt a sudden coldness run through me; she's met someone.

'I've met this wonderful man at work, he's gorgeous'

I knew it; here she was talking about a man, not boys but a man.

'His name is Callum Hughes; he's asked me out'

Her excitement was infectious, and I showed my delight but something troubled me. Her experience with boys was non-existent and now she was talking about a man. I feared for her but could not say anything. She was old enough to make her own mind up. Later, when she had washed her hair, I sat with her and cautiously asked if he knew about Mo being with me.

'He already knows that you live together' she calmly declared

'Already knows?

'Yes, I thought I'd better tell him before he got the wrong idea when he met you both'

Her forwardness did surprise me, but I had taught her to be open. It just seemed a bit quick to tell him. Charlotte hadn't planned for an 18th birthday party, but Mo suggested we now had one and this new man could be invited. It would make it less formal to meet him then. So, when the day came Charlotte was obviously impatient for him to appear. Many guests arrived but she spent little time greeting them and kept looking outside for him.

'Where is he?' she was getting quite anxious.

As he came into view, Charlotte raced towards him. Throwing her arms around his neck they embraced passionately.

'Where have you been, I thought you weren't coming?' Pulling his hand, led him into the house.

'This is my mother Elizabeth, and this is Maureen her friend'

He graciously shook both our hands and told us his name although Charlotte had mentioned him so often, we didn't need an introduction. Then, with a tug on his arm, she whisked him into the crowd hovering around the drinks bar erected in the back room. Mo looked at me over her new glasses and said

'That's a turn-up for the books'

I wasn't sure how to take that comment, but I knew how I was feeling at that moment. A feeling I'd last experienced when I met John for the first time. A desire to get to know him better, but reluctant to show it. My heart was racing, and I came over dizzy. The rest of the evening I kept my distance and busied myself serving drinks. I found it difficult not to keep an awareness of him and found myself staring at him more than once. He must have sensed this, and our eyes met several times. He's perfect, I thought, not for Charlotte but perfect for me. Later, as the guests started to leave, I began to clear up some of the glasses. Considering the cultured lot, they claimed to be, I thought they were still a very noisy and messy crowd. Callum was with a small group in the kitchen with Charlotte who hung on his every word. She had food spilt down her new dress and I knew it would need a good soak to get the mark out. Mo was getting tired and encouraged those remaining that it was home time. They thanked us and gave us full credit for a lovely party. Now with only us four left Mo pointed out the stain on Charlotte's dress.

'I'll just change it' she said to Callum

'Keep an eye on him for me mum, I'll be back in a moment'

With that, she ran upstairs with Mo. I was stacking plates on the sink edge and as I turned his face was in mine. I was taken by surprise and brought my hands up to my breast as if to protect myself.

'Thank you for a lovely evening, Elizabeth, I can see where Charlotte gets her beauty and poise from now'

His voice was mellow and very seductive. His eyes focused on me; it was as though he was looking into my soul. I wanted to take him straight to my bed. Reality then kicked in and I shuddered at how indecent this all was. He was forbidden fruit and it would be wrong to deceive Charlotte. Her choice of men was faultless so where had I gone wrong in the past?

As Charlotte returned, Callum asked if he could become a frequent visitor to see Charlotte, then added

'And to see you again of course'

Taking my left hand, he kissed my wedding finger gently. I melted and just nodded as he left the room. Is he for real? I thought. Mo entered the room as he kissed me and commented on my reaction.

'Felt something did you?'

I had but needed to remain true to Mo.

'The drink...., yes the drink, I must have drunk too much'

Mo just smiled at me and together we sneaked off upstairs. Charlotte was heard to come in and called up the stairs

'Thank you, Mum and Mo, see you in the morning'

Not too early I hoped, as it was Sunday.

# Chapter 10

During the next few months, Charlotte saw little of Callum as his job responsibilities increased. The times he had called at the house could be put on one hand and she hardly spoke of him. Charlotte had reservations about him and admitted that she had been crying last night when he failed to turn up as arranged. I secretly hoped that they would split up and I could stake my claim. How awful of me, I wanted him, but he wasn't free. Mo appeared to have forgotten my heart-fluttering moment when he came to the party, but I had not. I still felt an overwhelming desire for him. I kept saying to myself, what about the age gap? This did not shake any sense into me, and my desires grew stronger. One day he called at the house unexpectedly.

'I was just passing and thought I owed you a visit'

I ushered him into the living room and offered him a drink. Here he was in my house and alone with me. Maybe it was fate bringing us together.

'So, what has been happening lately, I have not seen much of you for ages' I asked, hoping he'd say he'd missed me.

'I've been very busy at work and the study course I am doing is taking up all my time'

I thought for a moment and after reminding myself he was Charlottes and that I should think of her, asked him if he missed seeing her?

He didn't hesitate and confirmed he would like to marry her.

'So, your intentions are honourable then?'

'Then why haven't you asked her yet?'

'I will when I've finished my degree'

A degree, he's not just good-looking but clever with it. The kettle boiled and I made us a drink. We took the cups into the living room, and I sat opposite him. We talked about many things, and I noticed he kept looking at my legs. I knew I had quite a shapely figure as Mo had told me my legs were long and jokingly led up to heaven. Here he was probably thinking the same. It all became too much for me and I asked him candidly

'Do you think I've got nice legs?

He didn't shy from answering

'If you weren't Charlotte's mother, then I think you would be my ideal woman'

I squirmed on the seat and became embarrassed. I hadn't expected a reply such as that and I no longer felt in control of the conversation.

'Well, I must get on now; it was nice to see you'

I almost threw him out, but something told me this didn't end there. He waved to me from the gate, and I closed the door.

When Charlotte came home, he telephoned her. She washed and dressed quickly and without telling me anything left the house. Later, that evening she returned and had obviously been crying.

'What's the matter?' I asked nervously

'He's done it'

'Done what? I asked, thinking the worst.

'He's asked me to marry him'

She lifted her hand and showed me the enormous ring he'd given her. Her face lit up and she began crying again. These were tears of joy; not of upset as I'd thought. I congratulated her and wished her future went well. How could I not think that this was my daughter's big chance of true happiness but underneath my smiling face, I kept my secret wish to myself. I went to bed that night and Mo said she was feeling horny after hearing the good news so we made slow and sensual love, but all I could think of was, why had I not seen him first and not Charlotte? Over the next few months, Callum came to the house more often. On one such visit, Charlotte asked if he could stay over as they were both leaving at lunchtime to travel to the coast for a short break to celebrate his getting a good exam result. I agreed and Mo suggested we start the celebrations tonight. We opened several bottles of wine, and a bottle of brandy came out of the cupboard for the first time in ages. The conversation was fresh and the mood convivial. Midnight was soon upon us, and everyone slipped off to bed. Mo went straight to sleep but I lay there thinking I should have gone to the toilet before getting into bed.

Finally, I gave in to the pressure and slipped out of bed; I usually slept naked, so wrapped a small towel around myself and went to the bathroom. As I sat down to relieve myself, I realised how much I needed a wash. So, there I was in the middle of the night having a warm shower, it felt good. After drying myself with the small towel I placed it in the laundry basket and thinking that everyone else was fast asleep stepped out of the bathroom. To my amazement, there stood Callum, waiting to use the bathroom. He was stark naked as well. It was obvious he was very intoxicated and propped himself up against the wall.

'Heard someone using the shower, so I waited' he said

I stood there momentarily as he looked at my glistening body; squinting as though he couldn't focus. I didn't want to be found in this compromising position, as it wouldn't be seen as an innocent encounter. I began to pass him, and he moved sideways into my path, so I stepped back. It was then I realised he had an erection and God it looked inviting. I stood for what seemed a lifetime, just admiring his body.

Eventually, I did manage to pass him but as I did so, I ran my fingertips along the length of his penis. He flinched and fell into the bathroom. I got back into bed and played with myself as Mo slept soundly by my side. The next day we all had a late breakfast. Charlotte and Callum went off for their holiday at about eleven thirty leaving Mo and me to spend the rest of the day cleaning the house. Callum hadn't looked at me before he went, so either he was too shy to say anything, or he couldn't remember a thing, probably the latter. Charlotte had left me with some good news, that she was pregnant. I wasn't to say anything until she had told Callum while they were away.

When they returned, I couldn't wait to tell Mo. She was excited at first but after a while went for a walk down by the canal on her own. I knew she was thinking about her situation and the fact she may never become a mother herself. Later, Mo came back and remarked how she was comforted by the tranquillity of the Wharf. I knew this was the case, as I had often spent time there when I needed to settle my thoughts.

On Saturday morning, Mo took Charlotte into town and left Callum at home with me. He told me that the house walls were closing in on him and he needed to get out somewhere. I took him to the canal, and we sat for about an hour talking about Charlotte and his future with her. He explained that he loved her a lot but there was something missing.

'Maybe with the baby on the way you might find your love grow stronger'

I said this to try and make him feel better, but he didn't see that it would alter how he felt. He didn't know what the matter was but was open to suggestions as he wanted to be happy with his life.

'You're going to be fine, I'm sure of it'

As I finished speaking, he burst into tears, so I moved closer to comfort him. I placed my arm around his shoulder and pulled him towards me. He turned slightly and we hugged each other. My mind was in turmoil. I had waited for so long to be in his arms and lost much sleep over him. Now though, I knew my affection would be purely maternal. We clung to each other for some time, and I began to realise he wasn't holding me like at the beginning. His hands were feeling my body and he'd stopped crying. I felt different as well and let him move me down onto the grass, as he rolled to my side. He kissed me gently on the forehead and I thought that it was his way of thanking me for being there for him. But no, I was very wrong. He brought his hand across my waist and held me firmly as he kissed me on the lips. Not a gentle kiss but a strong assertive kiss. Something like the ones you give when passion is raging in your loins. What was he doing? I thought. But I didn't want him to stop. He needed comfort and I could give it to him. Here and now if that's what he wanted.

With no thought of the time or the place, we made fast and furious love. After a while, I nudged him and suggested we make our way back to the house. We never spoke after that and later when the other two arrived back from town I told them we'd sat watching a video.

'Oh, which one?' asked Mo

I didn't expect an enquiry so was stumped for an answer.

'You won't believe it, but I fell asleep throughout'

'Well Callum, what did you watch? asked Charlotte.

He looked up and repeated almost word for word what I'd used as a lame excuse that he had fallen asleep.

'A fat lot of good you two are'

Quickly, I jumped up and offered to make a drink. Charlotte sat with Callum, and they cuddled until I returned with the drinks.

'So, apart from sleeping through the film, what else did you get up to' asked Mo

I looked at Callum and he looked at me. We both tried to speak at the same time but faltered. So, I told her we'd talked about the new baby Charlotte was carrying and what a joy it was to expect the patter of tiny feet. We all smiled at the thought. I caught Callum looking at me several times throughout the evening and I discretely winked at him.

We made every effort to conceal our affair in the weeks that followed and spent many hours together, knowing that Charlotte had gone off the idea as her belly grew bigger. Callum still had manly needs; so, I fulfilled them. Sex with him was different from my time with Mo. She catered for my other specific needs of gentleness which a man doesn't seem to appreciate. So, I had the best of both worlds; how lucky could anyone be? I didn't feel guilty towards Charlotte or Mo as I knew if I kept it a secret no-one would be the wiser and get hurt. There were times when I thought it would come out though. Charlotte had a bad time during the last few weeks of her pregnancy and became paranoid about the way I was always flirting with Callum.

'You're always doing it' she said accusingly

'Doing what?'

'You know, the way you talk to him, always goading him with innuendo'

'You're imagining it darling' I said trying to reassure her.

'Well, I wish you wouldn't'

I knew I'd overstepped the mark and told Callum to behave in her company in future. He said it was difficult being in love with two people, particularly as they were mother and daughter.

My time with Callum was conducted in many different places, in the kitchen, on the hallway mat, in the garden shed, and everywhere the mood took us. We could hear Mo and Charlotte in the house when we were at it in the shed but now thought it was too dangerous; Charlotte was so suspicious. I suggested we would only have sex down at the canal, as this was a quiet place where we could be ourselves. This we did and must have lain on every blade of grass in our special corner; they were wonderful times.

Our happiness was brought to a sudden halt one day by a large dog sniffing at our feet. I jumped up and pulled my clothes into some order. The owner of the dog called out. The dog ignored him and carried on wagging its tail, so I called back to the man

'He's over here'

I wasn't aware that Mo was walking up behind him. Apparently, she was looking for me and seeing my half-dressed state came over. I quickly moved away from Callum and told him to stay down. He didn't understand why and stood up. His trousers were still unbuckled, and Mo realised what we'd been doing. She turned and went back to the house. Together, Callum and I followed her. I immediately went upstairs where Mo was pulling things out from under the bed.

'Where's the fucking suitcase?' she raged at me.

I tried to speak but she was having none of it. Within 10 minutes she had packed a few things and was out of the house and along the lane. Charlotte was at the hospital having a check-up so missed her departure. Callum suggested Mo would be back and would probably not say anything to Charlotte. I hoped that would happen.

Later, Charlotte came home in a taxi; usually, she caught the bus. Callum met her at the gate, paid the driver and helped her inside. She was obviously distressed and needed his arm for support.

'What's the matter?' I asked as Callum placed a cushion behind her back.

With tears starting to flow she explained that the baby was not developing properly and there was a risk of miscarriage.

'What even at this late stage?' I asked

'Yes, they're very concerned'

Callum didn't know what to think and went into the kitchen to put the kettle on.

'I'm sure things will be all right for you darling, you wait and see'

I was not certain of it but thought it might calm her. The next day Callum took Charlotte shopping, I stayed at home hoping Mo may come back, but she didn't and a man in a white Bedford van called to pick up the rest of her stuff. She'd gone for good. With Mo out of my life, I could see Callum more often. It still felt right as Callum and I got the sex that we wanted, Charlotte was content with the prospect of motherhood, and I enjoyed seeing them happy. Unfortunately, this utopian life was to fall apart. Callum received some bad news and was summoned to his parent's hometown by the police. They were not able to tell him much, but his presence was urgently required. Not wanting to speculate on what was happening he told us not to worry and that he would be unlikely to return this evening, so not to cook anything for him. Kissing Charlotte on the lips and me on my cheek he left for the railway station.

Charlotte had only met his parents once when he announced their engagement. I hadn't travelled to see them and only spoke on the telephone when they rang to say thank you for having such a beautiful and charming daughter; a credit to me. The evening meal was a simple salad using the last of the lettuce and tomatoes from the little greenhouse that I'd made from old windows. It gave me the chance to use up the remains of the roast chicken from Sunday and Charlotte made a rhubarb and apple crumble. It was almost 11 o'clock that night when the telephone rang. Charlotte picked it up on the extension in her bedroom. I was desperate for a wee so continued along the landing to the bathroom. I hadn't closed the door when she gave out a loud cry of distress. Thinking she had hurt herself I rushed to her side. Still holding the phone, I took it from her and asked who was there. Callum spoke and told me the devastating news. His parents had been involved in a collision with a fuel tanker and before they could escape were enveloped in flames as the load caught fire. He was concerned about Charlotte and would ring again tomorrow. I assured him I would look after her and gave him our love. Cuddling her for what seemed ages I was reminded by the pressure on my bladder why I was going to the bathroom. I slowly unravelled myself and left her. When I returned, I found her curled up with her pillow, fast asleep. I covered her with a blanket and crept out of the room. I managed to get some sleep but by morning I had a thumping headache, so went downstairs to find Charlotte already pouring a cup of coffee.

'Here you have it; I forgot myself and put sugar in it'

She always made Callum a cupper and took it up to him early so he could have a lay-in; only today he wasn't here.

'Are you not having one' I asked as I rummaged through the drawers for some paracetamol.

'No, I'm going for a shower, maybe later'

Sitting in my dressing gown I began thinking of how painful this must be for Callum. I wanted to be there for him, but he was far away.

We always shared our deepest thoughts, and this sustained us when feeling down. Now though, he was alone.

By the time she returned my head was feeling better and I put the kettle back on.

'What if he's not back by Wednesday, my due date, I do want him to be there' she said hopefully

'Let's hope so, are you ready for a coffee yet?'

The morning passed slowly, and few words were spoken by either of us. The silence was broken about lunchtime with the telephone ringing. This time I got there first, and it was Callum, so I passed the phone to Charlotte. After she came off the phone, she explained that he couldn't get home until Monday evening and would ring again as he was leaving. This upset her and she began to cry. Moving into the garden we sat by the rose arch and as I handed her my handkerchief she scathingly said

'Never asked how I was.... or the baby'

Realising how his thoughts were with his departed parents I reassured her he wasn't thinking properly now. Nothing seemed to help how she was feeling but after several minutes eventually calmed

'Well, maybe your right'

Monday soon arrived and Charlotte greeted him at the gate. I stood back and kept out of view as they needed each other right now. As I placed a couple of frozen meat pies in the oven, they entered the kitchen

'Bet you are hungry after all that travelling?' I said

'Well yes, I suppose I am'

I wanted to hold him, to tell him I'd missed him and share his pain, but I would have to wait until we were alone. It seemed an eternity before Charlotte went up to bed and settled. The relief on his face was obvious and he gave me a warm and loving cuddle.

'I've missed you terribly' he said as I realised, he sported a bulge in his trousers.

'I can see that'

Stroking his nose with the forefinger of my left hand, undid his belt with my right. It was worth waiting for. The next day at breakfast, Charlotte clutched at her bump and screamed with pain. I called an ambulance and Callum followed in the car. She was taken straight into the delivery room at the hospital and while we sat outside Callum held my hand discreetly under his coat.

'Are you excited?' I asked

'Yes, I think so'

'Think so, is that the best you can do?'

I could see he wasn't enjoying the moment and wondered whether he questioned where his loyalties lie.

An hour passed and nothing seemed to be happening, so we went to the cafe by the hospital entrance, run by volunteers. After buying a drink a nurse came in and told us that Charlotte was asking for us. Leaving the drinks on the table the three of us returned to the room. Entering we expected to see her holding a baby, but Charlotte began screaming out repeatedly that she was sorry. As Callum tried to comfort her, the nurse ushered me out into the corridor. She explained that the baby had been born asleep. I was devastated. Charlotte had also told Callum and I could hear him sobbing. I waited a short while, composing myself before joining him at her side. I stroked his hair and resting my hand on his shoulder leaned forward and kissed her on the forehead.

'I'll wait outside if you want to be alone, darling'

'No mum, please stay'

Callum wasn't being much help and offered me his chair. He pulled another from behind the door, sat down, placed his head in his hands and continued sobbing. The nurse called for a porter, and they helped us all into a room off the ward where we could grieve in private. A doctor came later and after offering his condolences insisted Charlotte remained in the hospital overnight and instructed the nurse to give her a sedative to help her sleep. Callum and I stayed until 8 o'clock, although not asleep yet Charlotte looked awfully tired as the medication was taking effect, so we said our goodbyes and left the room. Looking back through the glass panel in the door I could see her heavy eyes close. Callum and I slept in our own separate rooms, even though it was the first time we were alone overnight. This would have been a welcome situation any other time, but now I couldn't stop thinking of Charlotte and I know Callum was thinking the same.

Over the next two days Charlotte remained in the hospital and after allowing her time to get over the initial shock gave her some more bad news; not that she needed anymore. The checks they carried out after the stillbirth of her baby boy, now given the name Peter, were to confirm that she had a problem with her womb and that it was unlikely she could carry another baby to full term. When she came home and told us, Callum was beside himself and unable to think clearly, so he went down to the canal. Normally I would have gone with him, but I knew this would be difficult for him after losing his parents earlier, so I stayed with Charlotte and offered her all the support I could.

# Chapter 11

In the days that followed we all crept about solemnly, not wanting to upset the calm and serene atmosphere that filled our house. Callum made the arrangements to bury little Peter. It was a quiet funeral and only a few people were asked if they wanted to attend the service. The day after I returned to the grave and placed a small wooden cross until a permanent stone could be ordered. It was almost another month before Callum received word about collecting his parents. He was in no state of mind to make further funeral arrangements, so a close friend of his parents was asked to assist. Charlotte and Callum went to the funeral in Nottingham a week later, but I stayed at home. I'd never met his family and the journey didn't appeal to me as I'd been quite poorly recently. Whilst they were away I did rather a stupid thing and tried to change a light bulb at the top of the stairs; I came over faint and fell all the way down. I was lucky to not be unconscious and managed to crawl to the telephone. Blood was pouring from a big gash on my head and my left arm seemed to be out of shape. As I sat in the cubicle of the accident department, I didn't think much damage had been done but after sewing up my head wound and encasing my arm in plaster, I realised how stupid and how lucky I was. What will the kids think of me? Kids, I had called Callum a kid, but he was my lover, how could he be a kid? This was the first time I'd ever really questioned my actions. Before I could analyse my feelings, the Doctor came through the curtain screen and introduced himself. He stood reading a piece of paper attached to a clipboard for ages.

'You were very lucky, Ms Yates'

I wasn't sure whether he was being sarcastic as I lifted my sling to show him. He laughed and said cheerfully

'No, you're lucky you didn't harm your baby'

I'm sure he said something about my baby, but I'm not pregnant, how could he be talking about me.

'I'm sure you're mistaken, I'm.....'

Interrupting, he confirmed there was no mistake

'These are your notes and your X-rays'

Smiling at me, he told the nurse I could be released. On the journey home in the taxi, I tried to remember when and how this could have happened. I knew how these things happen but when? Then I remembered. The night I'd drank so much I could hardly stand. Callum had cornered me as I took some fresh air in the garden. We'd made love behind the hedge at the back of the property. I didn't need this right now.

When at home I could see the answer phone machine flashing and pressed the replay button. It was from Charlotte saying they were staying over for a few days to sort out his parent's property and its contents. It ended with her saying she loved me so much and would see me soon. I didn't need to hear her say things like that; she loved me so much when I was expecting her fiancés baby. At least I had some time to figure out what to do; how to explain my being pregnant. Should I tell Callum? He had a right to know, but they had lost little Peter so how would he feel now that I was expecting? My mind was spinning, so I poured a brandy and sat curled up in the armchair trying not to explore too many questions that had no answers. A few days later Charlotte and Callum turned up unannounced.

'Thought you might have called to let me know you were coming back'

'We thought we'd surprise you'

'But I've nothing in for tea'

'That's alright we had something on the train, just a sandwich but it was all we needed'

Callum hadn't been listening, so she nudged him to agree but all he did was give her a funny look and went out to bring in some more boxes from the gate where the driver had just dumped them.

'Gosh, there's a lot of stuff here' I said, surprised they had managed to carry so much

'Yes, it's all from Callum's old bedroom'

After bringing in the last of the bags and boxes Callum asked for a drink of squash and settled down in my armchair. The empty brandy glass still at the side caught his eye.

'Secret drinker now, are we?' as he looked at me. Charlotte told him I was entitled to a drink if I liked, as it was my house, although she gave me an unfavourable look as well.

'We'll sort that lot out tomorrow if that's alright with you mum'

Callum agreed and said he wanted an early night. When they had gone upstairs, I expected Callum to sneak back down but he didn't, and I was left to contemplate what boyhood memories were in those bags. Letters from girlfriends, souvenirs from day trips to the seaside, bits of string he'd saved for emergencies and all sorts of other rubbish. I was soon in bed myself and lay still wondering how I would explain my pregnancy. I decided not to tell either of them yet as I didn't show at all. I needed time to get it right, I'd kept so many secrets before, another one wouldn't make any difference.

The next day I came downstairs early and sat in the garden watching the sun break through the trees. I heard Callum in the kitchen so approached the back door as he began to step outside with two cups of coffee.

'Got your hands full I see; I can do whatever I like, and you can't stop me'

'Not now Charlottes awake upstairs'

'Well remember this is still yours' as I opened my dressing gown to expose my nakedness. His eyes popped out and almost dropped the coffee.

'Where's my coffee, I thought you were coming straight back'

Charlotte was behind him. I turned quickly and tied up my gown. I couldn't face her; had she seen me tempting her man?

'Make mum a cup of her own, she's not having mine'

Coffee, my god she's talking about the coffee.

'Don't worry I'm going for a shower' and I slipped past them both and went upstairs.

After that nerve racking moment earlier, I kept a low profile and later went for a walk on my own. I sat on the bank down by the canal. What if she'd caught me? I keep thinking about it and doubts kept telling me to end the affair. Back at the house they had started unpacking the rubbish bags. Sorry, I mean the special things of Callum's past.

'Look at this mum' she was holding up a picture of Callum doing a wee into a watering can, aged about 3 years.

'Hasn't changed a lot' I said as he threw a bundle of clothes at me.

'Here sort these out for me; they can go to a charity shop if they're any use'

Charlotte picked up a toy gun and started waving it about

'Any more from you two and I'll shoot your heads off'

We were all laughing and joking, a far cry from the previous few weeks and months. I checked each item carefully and folded them neatly in a pile. The last thing was a woollen shawl and I held it to my face and remembered a similar one I'd had for my first born. As I began to fold it, I saw the embroidered corner; it had my initials. This was mine but why was it here with Callum's stuff. My stomach began to ache and asked him

'Where is this shawl from?'

'Oh, it belonged to my real mother'

I thought my head would explode.

'Real mother?'

'Yes, I was adopted as a baby; apparently my real mother didn't want me so gave me up'

Dumbfounded by what I'd heard I excused myself and went up to my room. I could hear Charlotte asking him why he'd never mentioned about being adopted to her.

'Never thought of it before, always loved my parents as though they were my own'

He didn't think it mattered. It mattered to me. If ever I dismissed feelings of guilt before then, now I certainly couldn't. The child I'd brought into this world could be my lover. I reached for the wastepaper bin by the side of the bed and vomited. Charlotte came to my door

'Are you alright mum, you sound awful?'

'I'm alright, just give me a minute'

I lay on my bed too shocked to cry. Those hours of ecstasy I'd spent with him, everything had been so perfect and now I felt like killing myself. How could I have been so stupid and not ask more of his past. I was taken in by him from our first meeting and put aside any questions. All because I wanted him for myself. If only Charlotte hadn't met him. I knew now it must end and never tell him who he was to me. I certainly couldn't tell him about the baby within me. I composed myself and went downstairs. Keeping this pretence wasn't going to be easy, so after a short while I asked him if he could help me decide what to do with the last remaining piece of ground in the garden. He'd been interested in how it was taking shape.

'Yes, go and help mum, it will take your mind off things'

'Ok, won't be long'

As we left the room I began talking

'Not sure whether I should have a wildflower patch'

As we stepped out into the overcast garden rain clouds moved ominously across the sky. Looking at me very suspiciously Callum asked

'What's all this about then?'

'Well, I've come to a decision about us'

'Us, what do you mean?'

'Yes, us, we've got to stop seeing each other and I mean it before you say anything else'

'But what about how you feel towards me?'

Knowing it would hurt him more but realising it would help with the break-up I told him I'd never really loved him; it was only the sex. He wasn't happy and stormed off to the canal. I didn't follow and went back into the house.

'Where's he gone now?'

'I'm not sure darling, maybe to look at the wildflowers along the canal bank'

'Daft, that's what he is'

It was ages before he came back and went straight upstairs for a shower. Charlotte had forgotten his erratic behaviour and never asked why he went walkabout. The next day Charlotte and I went to town for some shopping therapy and girlie time. We had a great time, but my thoughts still weighed heavy on my mind. Several hours past and we made our way home. As I put down the things, I'd bought, Charlotte called out from her room

'Look, the wardrobe is empty, Callum's clothes have all gone' then laughing said

'Goodness he wasn't joking about the charity shop'

I knew different, he had gone. Just like Mo he'd had enough of my lies and deceit. After looking properly, realized he'd only taken his best clothes and had left. She didn't seem that bothered and just hugged me tightly and said

'At least we've got each other and who needs men anyway?'

Weeks later, I came up with a reason for my pregnancy. Charlotte was very surprised and only queried why I'd not mentioned it before; about meeting a man in Truro, Cornwall months earlier when I was on a short break. I told her I didn't even know his name.

'I didn't think you were like that'

'Well, just because I lived with Mo didn't make me a lesbian'

'Oh, so what does it make you then?'

'A woman with needs, just like you'

'Sorry mum but I'm not like that at all, sex never bothered me'

I already knew that and briefly thought of Callum. Again, I was disgusted with myself and changed the subject.

'Let's not talk about men anymore, you were right the other day; we don't need them'

I knew as I was saying this to Charlotte that it wasn't true, I did need loving, both kinds. The comforting cuddles when feeling down and having someone to come home to. And the physical side when you ache down there. Both my lovers had gone, and I contemplated my empty existence. Charlotte wouldn't understand if her idea of sex was a dull and routine affair designed to make babies. It was hardly surprising Callum went for me in that way. Now though, I didn't see anything good from knowing him. But he could be my son, and nothing could change that.

# Chapter 12

As my size grew Charlotte became very attentive and made sure I didn't strain myself doing chores around the house and garden. She caught me carrying a box of apples from the garden shed one day and I never heard the last of it. She was more anxious than me and I still wasn't sure whether I wanted to have the baby. Its little feet were kicking so I began to consider having it adopted. Charlotte would not like the idea, but it seemed the only answer. I dwelled on morbid thoughts and constantly reminded myself what a mess my life had been. How my mother had suffered years of bullying and when freedom was there for the taking, she died from cancer. I needed her then, as my own life was beginning, and the boys came knocking. Maybe I wouldn't have given myself up so willingly if she had been there to give me the love I needed. Auntie was there but I could not get close to her. I stumbled from one mistake to another, never learning anything. Charlotte was the only thing that had been perfect, and I even spoilt that by taking her man behind her back. I was part of the reason he'd left her; his parents dying and then his son born asleep. This was too much for him to handle. Whatever my thoughts were now, I needed to be there for Charlotte.

On the day my baby was due the midwife commented on how Charlotte was a comfort; the way she fussed after me. I felt guilty as I carried the burden of deceiving her. I was having Callum's baby and she was supporting me; it didn't seem right. As my baby entered the world Charlotte cried out

'He's got jet black hair'

She took him from the midwife momentarily while I was cleaned up. Then Charlotte laid him across my swollen breasts. Her outstretched arms not wanting to part with him. I remember how I felt when at 'Sunnyhill' and gave up my first baby. Tears filled her eyes and she turned away from me. I was so ashamed and now being rewarded by a beautiful son seemed so unfair.

In the weeks that followed she attended to almost everything except feeding him. The way she washed him, the clothes that she picked for him to wear, and at night kept vigil over him. She was a perfect mother. Since giving birth I'd felt very low, and the Doctor told me I had Post Natal Depression. Further tests were ordered, and I was called back to the surgery a few weeks later to discuss the findings. He told me that the tests were inconclusive but his colleague at the hospital would have another look at my results. I didn't wait long for an appointment and was soon in the waiting room of Mr. Mahmud, a consultant. The nurse kept sticking her head around the door and apologised for him being delayed in surgery, but it didn't matter. I had nothing else to do today as Charlotte looked after David; yes, I'd named him after my first crush. I did wonder why a surgeon would be asked for an opinion though. Eventually, he arrived and soon had me going for a scan.

'I'll need time to look at the results so come and see me a week from today, my nurse will make another appointment'

Still a little concerned I went home. Charlotte was in the kitchen, so I quickly looked in on David, who was sleeping soundly.

'How did it go then?' she asked as I sat down at the table.

'More tests I'm afraid, don't think they know what they're doing'

Not answering she poured the tea. David wakes up and starts crying. I'll go in to get him, he's due a feed. As I begin to pick him up, he screams louder. Charlotte tries to pick him up and he immediately stops crying and settles readily in her arms.

'There's a bottle of expressed milk in the fridge, he can have that, seeing as he doesn't want me'

It was obvious he thinks she was, his mother. I turn and leave the room and make my way down to the canal; there I'll collect my thoughts. Later that same week a telephone call from the hospital asked me to return before my scheduled appointment. Sitting in Mr. Mahmud's room again I start to worry. It wasn't without due cause as when he came in, he immediately gave me some shocking news. I had a cancerous lump in my left breast. Early intervention would be essential, so he booked me in for an operation the following week. Travelling home I made a decision that came very easily to me. I'd seen how David was with Charlotte and she with him. Having told her what was happening I went on to suggest she adopt him.

'But you're going to be alright'

'Well maybe I am, but it makes sense anyway'

We discussed the situation for hours and finally, she reluctantly agreed. It solved both our problems. She couldn't risk having another child even if she found another man. I was not bonding with David and now this other problem hung over me.

'Rather sort things out while we can'

'I still don't think it's that bad, they can do wonders these days' she said caringly

It was a busy week and it soon passed. I found myself looking at the ceiling as I waited to be pushed down to the operating room. A spider was building a web up in the corner and I thought of it losing its home the next time the cleaner came around with her duster on a long stick. The spider would rebuild the web and keep going. Comparing myself with it, I had to do the same. I had survived so far with all that life threw at me so this latest setback would be easy. The nurse alongside me tried to reassure me with comforting words as she pushed a needle into my arm. I began to slip into sleep and wondered if this was my punishment for the life that I had messed up. I needn't have worried, as the next day Charlotte was at my bedside praising how well I looked. I felt awful but I didn't let on. My chest ached so much, and it reminded me of how my father had punched my mother so many times before. David was sound asleep in her arms and plumping up my pillows with her free hand laid him alongside me.

'Can I get you something from the shop?'

'No thanks, maybe in a minute'

Later, while she was away a nurse came and introduced herself as being the surgeon's assistant during my operation.

'The doctor will be doing his rounds shortly'

Looking down at David's rosy cheeks he gave a big smile. I wasn't sure if he was dreaming or just had wind. Charlotte returned with a packet of chocolate fingers and some other nibbles.

'Best not eat them yet' I cautioned,

'The doctors due soon'

As predicted, he entered the room followed by at least eight young students all smartly dressed in white coats. Charlotte stood up and offered to leave but was quickly told not to concern herself as they would only be a minute. The doctor was softly spoken and pointing to the group asked

'Do you mind them being present?'

'No, it's fine'

He went on to explain in technical terms what he'd found and told me I should not have any problems again, but then said

'Fingers crossed'

This didn't sound like a guarantee but accepted that only time would tell. When they had gone, Charlotte spent about an hour with me. David did wake up but only for a few minutes before going back to sleep. She never mentioned what the doctor had said and assumed she wasn't concerned but I still felt unsure. It was at least a year after my operation that I was given all clear and things looked up for us all. The paperwork had been completed on David and Charlotte was in seventh heaven. My health improved dramatically, and I returned to work part-time at the local supermarket. Life couldn't be better. We never heard from Callum or Mo again and I hoped they managed to have a successful and happy life. I still missed them both but knew it would be too painful to see them again.

David's first birthday arrived, and a small gathering of my work friends was invited to attend his party. He was the centre of our world and I wanted to share our delight with them. Christine, a woman in her fifties but annoyingly only looked thirty admired David and commented how much he looked like his mother, Charlotte. I smiled and watched Charlotte's face knowing that this may cause her a problem. She was about to reply but another comment came from Mark, another work colleague who suggested he was probably the image of his father. I felt very uncomfortable, so invited everyone to top up their glasses for a toast. Charlotte stepped forward and gave a short thank you for the coming speech. Later, whilst everyone was getting ready to leave Charlotte asked about Mark and whether he was single. I had noticed him eyeing her up earlier and told her to see him in his car. This she did and they talked for ages by the gate; eventually he kissed her on the cheek and left. She came into the kitchen, picked up a black bag and began filling it with uneaten food and rubbish that seemed to have taken over the place.

'So, what do you think of him?'

'Seems a nice boy'

It was unusual for her to have so little to say.

'Come on, you know you fancied him'

'Maybe I did but that's my concern'

I took this to mean she was smitten with him and felt pleased for her. Since Callum had left, she hadn't spoken with many men, least of all gone on a date. I, on the other hand, had seen a few men but nothing serious; just for the sex. I had considered flirting with Mark previously and was pleased that I hadn't. Charlotte could make something of this, and I was not going to stand in her way this time.

Charlotte saw him a lot over the next few months and upon my suggestion they spent time down by the canal. I didn't ask what they got up to but knew it was a perfect place to get to know each other. I still fought my emotions about the times Callum spent with me laying on the long grass and the torment of finding out the truth about him. When Mark finally proposed to Charlotte I was overjoyed. At last, something good was happening to her, although the question of David still lingered in both our thoughts. Would she tell him or keep the secret as the grip of deceit took hold of her, as it did to me? They agreed to wait until David was old enough to act as page boy and Mark never queried where David's father was, so that made the situation easy.

# Chapter 13

Three years passed and the wedding was planned for the following Saturday. The local church was to be the venue, but it did look like a sorry state with overgrown weeds enveloping the walls outside and dirt and grime inside. Mrs. Cruikshank the cleaner was getting on in years and was unable to keep on top of the work. So, Mark and his friends spent two afternoons clearing the weeds and cleaning the place until it felt inviting. On the big day, David was the last to be dressed up in his outfit. He was like a magnet to dirt and never looked clean and tidy. Charlotte on the other hand was ready at least an hour before needed be.

'The bride is supposed to be late for the wedding'

'Yes Mum, but I'm not letting this one get away, so I'll be on time'

I wondered why she made such a comment but guessed it had something to do with Callum disappearing. Charlotte had grown up without a father so the role of giving her away was left to me, but everything else had been left to Mark to arrange. So, when a magnificent old Rolls Royce arrived outside, I was really surprised. I'd seen a car like it before in a movie but didn't expect one to pull up outside. After everyone else had left for the church, I stood by the door and called to Charlotte.

'It's time darling, we need to make a move'

She came down the staircase holding the train of her wedding gown. A truly beautiful sight with her silver shoes shining brightly like an evening star. I felt a tear run down my face. This was how I imagined a wedding should be, but I had never been part of one before. My own experience wasn't worth remembering. Now, seeing my beautiful daughter in all her finery made up for it. The journey to the church was slow and allowed us to talk a little. I gave her my best wishes and affirmed my belief that she would be happy with Mark and that David was so fortunate to get a father at long last. She leaned across and took hold of my hand, holding it tightly

'I know you will always be there for me'

I started to cry again, and she gave me her spare handkerchief. At the church, a small group stood waiting by the entrance. They scurried inside as we drew up leaving only the vicar's assistant to greet us. A man with a camera leapt out from behind a large stone monument and asked us to linger for a few photos. Finally, he let us move into the church. It was bedecked with a multitude of flowers and the scent wafted everywhere. I hoped that Mark had taken his allergy pill as he usually sneezed a lot during the summer when pollen was at its worst. The music struck up and we gracefully walked towards the front. David was ushered behind us and followed closely. Charlotte joined Mark at his side and David scattered petals around their feet from a small basket he carried. The vicar gave a wonderful service and after Charlotte uttered the words, I do, pronounced them man and wife. A kiss sealed the union, and everyone cheered. I had contained my emotions throughout but now sobbed uncontrollably. We all made our way back to the house and celebrated for hours. At about 9 o'clock Mark and Charlotte went among the guests thanking them for the presents that now littered the corner of the sitting room. Some were funny shapes and I wondered what the hell was inside the glossy paper. Mark had arranged a hotel room for a few nights by the coast and having put together an overnight bag they left as soon as they had thanked everyone again.

The next day I got stuck in and cleared up the house and managed to achieve great success. The place never looked better. So, after a small lunch and a glass of wine left from yesterday, I decided to sort through the spare bedroom. It hadn't been touched for ages and while I felt like cleaning this was the best chance I had to get on top of the mess in there. I started under the bed and pulled out all the boxes that hadn't been touched since Callum brought them from his parent's place. I expected to find more of his childhood junk after seeing some of it previously. To my surprise, I found a collection of photographs. I wasn't sure whether I should be looking at them, but curiosity got the better of me and I delved into them without a second thought. The photos were mainly of small children and a few of a young couple. I didn't recognise any of them, so it was helpful to see writing on the back of some. One caught my attention two small boys standing in front of an enormous cake with the word Happy 5th birthday across the top. On the back was written Callum and a date in the same month as my own baby was born. I was intrigued as the date didn't make sense. If it was Callum, then it would be his 6th birthday. I knew the month was correct for my son's birth, but it was a year out. I was confused and everything I thought I knew about him, and the blanket seemed in doubt. The blanket had indicated he could be my son, but the age is wrong. Maybe the age is correct, and the blanket wasn't his. The torment of not knowing drove me to distraction. What could I do? If I ask Charlotte, I would be raking up the past and Mark would not thank me for that. I resigned myself to not knowing and tried hard to forget the whole sordid affair. I'd lost interest in cleaning now and shoved the boxes back under the bed. I stormed downstairs and poured myself a large glass of wine and took a handful of unshelled peanuts from the bowl by the toaster. Eating had been my escape from reality in the past but recently I didn't need to. So now I felt guilty; God, I hate myself.

It wasn't long before Charlotte, Mark and David moved into one of the new houses built on the old milk depot land, just up the road from me. I saw them nearly every day and often collected David from school. He was growing into a little monster and needed plenty of control. I found it difficult to discipline him as Mark gave me such a glare when I'd said something before. I know I shouldn't say anything, but he was my son after all.

One afternoon David was playing in my garden whilst he waited for Charlotte to collect him. Suddenly he came running into the kitchen shouting loudly

'There's a man staring at me, there look he's by the gate' pointing as he pulled at my dress.

I dropped the potato peeler and grabbed a tea towel to dry my hands. I looked out and saw a scruffy man carrying a clipboard opening the gate. He was obviously a door-to-door salesman, and I was not of a mind to entertain his slick sales patter. Pushing David back inside the house I called out

'Sorry you're wasting your time; I don't want any today'

Undaunted, he closed the gate and walked towards me. Not knowing who or what he wanted I turned and closed the door. David was now sitting on the windowsill with his nose pressed up against the glass.

'Are you Mrs Yates?

I hesitated for a moment wondering whether to reply

'What if I am'

'Then my journey was not in vain'

He introduced himself as James Martin and that he was a genealogist looking for a family by the name of Hughes which I recognised was Callum's surname. I invited him in even though he still looked a bit shady in his dirty coat and unkempt hair. David crept from behind the settee and made faces at him.

'Excuse my son, I mean my grandson he's a bit of a sod'

I offered him a drink and handing a glass of water to him he sat down on the edge of the chair by the fire.

'So, why are you looking for the Hughes family?'

He told me about the accident and that a firm of solicitors had dealt with the family estate. They had not found anything of value to distribute amongst the descendants and had closed the account. However, it now transpires that the parents owned a property in

France. It was quite valuable so the solicitor having been unable to locate the two boys engaged him to find them. I was sure he said the two boys and queried

'Did you say two boys?'

'Yes, they had two adopted sons, Callum and Colin'

This was a shock to me; Callum had forgotten to tell us about being adopted and now we discover he had a brother as well. How many more secrets are to unfold I thought?

'This brother of Callum's, have you found him yet?'

'Yes, that's how I got your details'

'How did he know about us, if we never knew he existed?'

Apparently, Callum had written to his brother just after he'd met a new girlfriend and mentioned where we lived. He'd described a woman who had raven black hair with a silver streak at the front. I knew this dishevelled man was describing me, so I changed the subject and continued to ask about Colin. My questions were answered but all I could think of was the fact that Callum spoke to his brother about me and not Charlotte. He must have been obsessed with me from the very beginning, long before we got together. When I'd explained that Callum no longer lived here and didn't leave a forwarding address the meeting finished, and I asked for a contact telephone number for Colin. James reluctantly gave the details and left. David jumped up from behind the settee and startled me.

'Who was that?'

'It doesn't concern you, young man'

Just then Charlotte came into the room.

'Who was that, shutting the gate?'

'Oh, I'll tell you later, right now though I think we should have a nice cup of tea'

Charlotte left soon after and didn't ask again. Pouring myself another cupper I sat in the garden on the old tree that had fallen during the strong winds last year. Mark had carved a flat area to make it a bench seat rather than chop it up and use it for the fire. He was practical like that and often did little jobs around my house. Sipping the tea, I thought over the news of Callum having a brother. It raised so many questions. Should I contact Colin? Should I tell Charlotte? Did I really need to know anything about him? I had tried to forget the past, but this revelation stirred up everything for me. The picture under the bed did show another young boy so maybe he was Colin. The question had plagued me for ages about the blanket and I speculated that it could have been Colin's. Could he be my son?

Two days later I plucked up the courage and found myself dialling the number. A woman answered and I hesitated for a moment.

'Hello, is anyone there?'

'Err.., yes.., I'm sorry to bother you but is this the number for Colin?'

'Yes, it is, who's calling?'

I felt very uneasy and explained he didn't know me, but I was ringing about his brother Callum. The phone sounded like it had been dropped and went quiet. A man came to the phone and introduced himself as Colin and urgently said

'Callum, you know where he is?'

'No, not exactly'

He sounded quite disappointed, as he obviously wanted news of him.

'I'm sorry but I haven't seen or heard of him for nearly four years'

'Well, why are you calling?'

He listened as I explained that Callum had left some of his belongings at my house. We agreed to meet up but as we lived quite distant from each other a halfway point was suggested. Coming off the phone I poured the biggest brandy I've ever had and drank it almost in one go. I shuddered and fell back into my chair. My thoughts were still mixed up but at least I may find out the truth soon. The wait was agonising. I didn't confide in Charlotte what I was doing so couldn't discuss it with her. On that day, I travelled to the train station by taxi. Unfortunately, I arrived there late and missed the through train. I waited ages for the next one and this gave me time to go over all the questions I would ask Colin. The train eventually arrived, and I was on my way. Being almost an hour late I wasn't sure whether he would be there. As I turned the corner of the station entrance a woman approached me and asked if I was Elizabeth Yates. Having kissed my cheek, we walked along the road to a nearby pub. Stepping inside I looked around and found the place almost empty. Nobody even resembled Colin. I turned to the woman who I now knew as Kirstie, Colin's wife. She looked as surprised as me that he was not there. She was about to say something when he came out of the gent's toilet. We settled down by the bay window, it seemed so gloomy in the rest of the place. Built decades ago, it hadn't moved on with the times and Kirstie commented that the wallpaper was simply prehistoric. With a drink in front of us, I asked if they'd had a good journey and some other small talk.

'Well here we are then' Kirstie sighed

'Yes, here we are' I repeated

'So, what have you brought with you?' Colin seemed impatient to see what was in my suitcase.

I'd dragged the damn thing along for what seemed miles but was only a few hundred yards. Opening it on the table, he rummaged through Callum's memories. I waited until he'd finished and when he realised how little value had been there thanked me, but I sensed his disappointment.

'There is something else' I said encouragingly, as I pulled the bundle of photos from my pocket.

Handing them to him his eyes lit up and as he flicked through them smiled intermittently. This improved the atmosphere and I felt it was time to ask some of my questions.

'In the pictures, I noticed a young boy standing in front of a birthday cake'

He took it from the pile.

'Yes, that's Callum and that's me standing behind him'

'So, whose birthday, was it?'

'Callum's, mine was a week later but I don't see any photos of that, shame really as my cake was better by far'

I thought for a while and things started to fall into place. I'd assumed the other boy in the photo was older and asked Colin when he was born. He confirmed he was a year older. My feelings were quite emotional by now as it became a possibility that Colin maybe my son. Kirstie, seeing our almost empty glasses offered to get another drink and I asked for the same again. While she was at the bar, I asked Colin about the blanket. To my surprise and delight, he explained that as children they had both used the blanket.

'Firstly, I used it and when I outgrew the need for it Callum was given it'

I wanted to ask why Callum thought it was his and why he'd remarked about his parents not wanting him, but this was not the time. Colin was intrigued by my line of questions and asked why I was so interested. I hesitated for a moment before speaking.

'Well, you see I had a son in the same year that you were born but I've never seen him since he was adopted'

When I told him about the blanket and the embroidered inscription the colour seemed to disappear from his face. Before he could speak Kirstie came back with the drinks and seeing him in an apparent state of shock asked

'Are you all right darling, you look as though you've seen a ghost?'

He raised his glass and drank some of his beer. I repeated what I'd told Colin. Her reply was quick and excitedly asked

'Well, there's a surprise but is it true, could you really be his mum?'

I didn't know what to say and shrugging my shoulders just smiled at her. Turning to Colin she asked

'Well, what do you think?'

He agreed it was possible but still looked ill, his voice broken. Kirstie tells me that Colin had tried to find his real parents years ago but gave up when the system refused to tell him anything. Pressing him she asked

'You'd still like to know who your parents were?'

'Yes, I suppose so'

'You can have a new DNA test nowadays to establish whether you are related, why don't you both have one?'

Colin looked at me, smiled and then asked

'Would you mind?'

'No, I would like that'

Kirstie stood up again and leaned across the table giving me a hug and a kiss. Colin didn't move and continued to drink his beer. The meeting finished soon after and we all left the pub. I told him that he could keep the suitcase and he promised to look after it. They offered to escort me to the station, but I declined and after a handshake, we went our separate ways. I kept looking back until they were out of sight and on the journey home, I contemplated what a lovely son Colin would make for someone, even if it wasn't me. I didn't tell Charlotte about my meeting with Colin and Kirstie until after I had taken the tests. She was really surprised and happy for me but scolded me for not telling her sooner. It took about a month to get news from the clinic and as the postman handed me a brown envelope he said jokingly

'Good news I hope'

Little did he know how important the letter was and how it may affect us. Charlotte had been talking about the possibility of having a half-brother since I told her and was just as anxious to find out the results. As the postman closed the gate Charlotte arrived with David.

'Hi Mum, just called round for a cupper'

Still holding the letter, she asked if it was from the clinic.

'Don't know, haven't opened it yet'

David started to cry, and I picked him up. Charlotte took the letter from me and asked if she should open it.

'Yes, if you like'

She tore the end of the envelope and began reading it. Her reading was always slow, and I developed tenseness in my stomach. Her smile broadened as she gave me the news

'Mum, there's a match, a 99.9% match'

My tears started to flow as my anguish gave way to feelings of joy. Charlotte wrapped her arms around David and me. We hugged for ages until the telephone started to ring. Taking David from my arms Charlotte asked

'Are you expecting a phone call?'

'No'

'Well, you'd better answer it'

Slowly lifting the handset and bringing it to my ear I cautiously said 'Hello'

The voice I now knew was Colin's. He confirmed it was me and began to speak of the test results being due to arrive, but my mind was not open yet. I was still somewhere else. I listened a little more, then answered. I have the results; they have just arrived.

'Colin, you are my son'

There was no reply for a moment.

'Yes, I am your real mum' I continued.

Kirstie had now taken the phone off Colin and explained he had fainted. I told her what I had found out and she was overjoyed for him. He had now collected himself and took the phone again. He struggled to speak as he started to cry. I couldn't make any sense of what he was saying but knew how he felt.

Over the next few days, we spoke at length and tried to fill in the gaps. I was probably more than relieved than anyone realised in view of my indiscretions with his stepbrother, but it made everything right in a way.

Life would never be the same again.

# Don't miss out!

Visit the website below and you can sign up to receive emails whenever H J BURGESS publishes a new book. There's no charge and no obligation.

https://books2read.com/r/B-A-AYLY-RUMJC

Connecting independent readers to independent writers.

# Also by H J BURGESS

A Cornish Saga
Love and Belonging

www.ingramcontent.com/pod-product-compliance
Ingram Content Group UK Ltd.
Pitfield, Milton Keynes, MK11 3LW, UK
UKHW031852160225
455176UK00003B/5

9 798223 457237